FIXING YOU

ROYA CARMEN

COPYRIGHT

Cover design, formatting and illustration: Calico Images
Editing: CKMS Media
Follow Roya Carmen to keep in the loop about all the upcoming releases, sales and freebies.

Roya Carmen Goodreads
Roya Carmen Facebook Page

1

______

ACT YOUR AGE FOR A CHANGE

As fish flew at rocket-speed above Kirsten's head, she stood clustered between what seemed like a thousand tourists and realized the day was not turning out as expected. Seattle's famous Pike Place Fish Market. She had anticipated something a little more romantic. She lived and worked just a short walk away and she often came to the market for fresh ingredients to make dinner for her and her mother Lorraine. She loved Pike Place Market. But...

When Logan had suggested they do something special with a curious expression, she had gotten all kinds of excited. This was it, she thought. The big day. They had been together for almost five years... it was time. Logan was a sweetie, a corporate lawyer, handsome in a preppy way. She thought he was quite the catch.

But speaking of 'catch', she couldn't help but wonder if this wasn't quite the best suited location to pop the big question. Smelly men throwing slimy fish at each other? Perhaps not the most romantic spot in the world.

But who knew? Maybe he wanted to do it smack in the middle of a crowd to make things a little more exciting. Yet, that didn't quite seem like him. He was rather a straight-arrow, as straight as they come. This was fine as far as Kirsten was concerned. After all, she was quite the straight-arrow herself. And her chosen profession of Librarian only added to the whole picture. Good Girl. Bookworm. Straight Arrow.

She caught a quick glance of Logan and for the first time that day, he seemed to be enjoying himself, shouting along with the crowd. He had been acting weird and nervous all day, but Kirsten concluded that might have had a little something to do with the big impending question. Logan had not been himself lately. He was rather distant, an odd mix of miserable and happy. She inquired about his moods once or twice, and he told her it had to do with work.

He caught her staring at him and nudged her shoulder. "Let's get out of here."

She smiled wide. "Where to?"

"Up for a little twirl in the sky?" he asked, but the concerned expression on his face confused Kirsten a little. This must be it, she thought. How perfect. A proposal on the famous Great Wheel. She could hardly contain her excitement. She grabbed his hand. "I'd love it," she almost sang.

As they stood in line among tourists, she thought about her wedding day. What would her dress look like? Something sleek and classy, she concluded. And the flowers? Lavender and cream hydrangeas perhaps. Lavender for the bridesmaids. But who would her maid of honor be? She didn't really have a best friend. Her mother had taken on that role. As an only child, she had always been extremely close with her mom. And she also invested so much of her time with Logan, she hadn't had a chance to make friends in the past five years.

As they stepped into the gondola car, her attention was brought back to Logan. He still seemed very jittery and she almost felt sorry for him. It must be nerve-wracking to pop the big question, she mused. They huddled close on the seat, looking out at the beautiful Seattle skyline and Elliot Bay. It was gorgeous. What a wonderful idea, she thought. She was certain there was a small velvet box hiding in the inside pocket of his jacket. She wanted to reach in and grab it. All in due time, she thought. But as they moved higher and the ride moved along, Logan was still silent. And Kirsten started to wonder.

Finally, he turned to her. "Listen, Kirsten," he started, his expression completely serious. She was a tad surprised by his demeanor, but then again, Logan had always been the serious type. "You are such an amazing woman," he went on and her body stood to attention, wanting to rip the words out of his mouth. "You are beautiful," he told her. "You're extremely intelligent," he went on as his shoulders visibly slouched. "Any man would be lucky to have you."

Something was off. She couldn't quite put her finger on it... but he looked so miserable. If he was just about to ask her to marry him, why did he look like he had the weight of the world resting on his shoulders? Why wasn't he happier? More excited?

What?! Oh God... was he trying to end it? It almost sounded like it. But that couldn't possibly be it.

"Are you..." she ventured with wide eyes, "...are you trying to break up with me?" she asked, eyes welling up. "On the Great Wheel?"

He shook his head, completely flustered. "No, no," he insisted. "Of course not," he told her, swiftly jerking his gaze to the ocean. He did not utter another word, and neither did she.

Just as she was about to fall into sobs, realizing there was not going to be a proposal; no velvet box, no momentous hug, no tears of joy, the attendant helped them out of the gondola car. Logan suggested they go for something to eat. She was confused. He was acting so peculiar. At first, she was sure he would ask her to spend the rest of his life with him, and the next minute, he seemed on the verge of dumping her. What a roller coaster. Ferris wheels and roller coasters – she felt like she was at a theme park. A really crappy theme park.

They settled down on uncomfortable wrought iron chairs in a quaint Paris-themed crêperie. Logan suggested the place, knowing how Kirsten loved crêpes. Kirsten indulged in a strawberry filled crêpe covered with extra whipped cream. Hell, she needed it.

Logan stared down at the banana and Nutella crêpe in front of him, not touching it. He bit his lip. "Kirsten, I... I..." he started, stammering. "I lied earlier," he admitted. "The thing is... you were right."

She sat up straight, curious. "Right about what?" She desperately wanted to know what the hell was happening. "Please, be straight with me, Logan," she pleaded.

He swallowed hard. "You know how much you mean to me, Kirsten..." She knew from his expression that this was it; the moment she dreaded. He was breaking up with her. "But I've been thinking about it for a while now," he struggled to add, "and I'm not sure I see you and me together in the future." He stared down at his untouched crêpe when he added, "I'm just not sure you're the one for me."

Her heart sank. It felt like a dead weight pressing against her stomach. As she realized she was still holding her fork mid-air, the smell of strawberries filled her nostrils. This didn't make sense. Why now? So suddenly. Why? There had to be an explanation.

"Is there someone else?" she whispered. As upset as she was, she didn't want to make a scene. But anger rose with every word coming out of Logan's mouth.

"Uh... no," he said, looking away. He picked up his fork and finally ventured a bite of his crêpe.

She knew him too well. She knew he was lying. Her voice rose when she scoffed, "You're lying."

He couldn't even look up at her when he confessed. "I'm sorry... yes, there's someone else," he admitted. "But it's not about her."

"Hell, it's not about her," she snapped. "What a bunch of crock."

"Who is she?" she asked, the possible culprits dancing around in her head. She couldn't pin one down. Logan had always been kind of stand-offish with women, only having eyes for her. Or so it seemed. Perhaps a woman from work?

"It doesn't matter," he said, finally looking up at her, his big brown eyes begging for her forgiveness. "Does it?"

"Hell, it does," she hissed. "The least you owe me right now is to give me the decency to tell me who it is."

He tilted his head, averting his gaze. He clearly did not want to get into this. But he really had no choice at this point. "Lisa," he finally offered. "We met at the yoga center."

Oh...

It all made sense now, looking back. The change in his attitude had started just about then, when he had started doing yoga. She had gone once but hadn't really enjoyed it. She was a little too tense and wired to really get into it. She had actually been surprised when he seemed to enjoy it so, never missing a class. It didn't quite seem to fit. But now it was clear as day. What he was really enjoying was the view.

"Someone in your class?"

He bit his lip. "Actually... the instructor," he offered, the last word trailing like a lost thought.

Hell, no.

He might as well have punched her in the gut. A yoga instructor? She remembered the woman and her tall tanned body, easy smile, and perky ponytail. Kirsten couldn't have been more different than this yoga goddess, even if she tried. "The one with the navel piercing and butterfly tattoo on her shoulder?" She still couldn't believe it. She needed confirmation.

Sheepish, he nodded.

She looked down at her half-eaten crêpe. The whipped cream was melting slowly but still there. Plenty left... she desperately wanted to shove her plate in his face. But she had never been one to make a scene. She would hurt him with words instead.

"I don't see it," she offered with a smirk. "You and her," she added with a constructed laugh. "You're so different... it'll never work. She'll be bored with you before the seasons change."

He swallowed hard. "Don't be like this," he scoffed. "I love her. And I'm crazier about her than I've ever been about you."

The words really hit her hard and as much as she was trying to retain her composure, she just couldn't any longer. Tears trailed to her cheeks, and she couldn't even look at him.

"I'm sorry, Kirsten," he told her. "I didn't mean that."

She grabbed her bag. "But you did," she cried. "I know you did."

And with those words, she walked out of the crêperie, not quite steady on her sensible chunky-heeled Mary-Janes.

As she waited for an elevator up to the suite she shared with her eccentric mother, she held her head high, trying to temper her emotions. She would absolutely not lose it in public. She stared at her blurry reflection in the stainless steel elevator doors, a well-put together woman with sensible black trousers, a pink sweater, brown hair in an up-do, and sleek hipster glasses.

What the hell was wrong with him?

I'm hot, damn it, she thought. Perhaps a little conservative, she amended, but some men like that. As she was scrutinizing her reflection, she spotted him creeping up behind her; the sleek designer suit, the sharp angles, the dirty blond hair.

Damn, she really didn't need this right now.

Ethan Fox. Seattle's most eligible bachelor. She didn't get it. Didn't get what the fuss was all about. Sure he was rich and gorgeous as sin, but he was such an arrogant wanker.

Sure, she had had that hot dream about him, once or twice. In the steamy dream, he had her pressed against a huge billowy headboard and was doing sinful things to her. She was sure that was just her subconscious reacting to a serious shortage of sex. Lately, she and Logan hadn't been very close. And obviously her subconscious was not as discerning or intelligent as she was.

He stood tall next to her. She didn't bother turning her head. After the day she had just had, she had absolutely no patience for the likes of him.

"Hey shorty," he quipped.

She sucked in a long breath, desperately trying to hold on to the anger threatening to burst out, in all kinds of directions. "Kirsten Beals," she said, the words clipped. "Like I've mentioned before... I have a name," she added, staring straight ahead at the people exiting the elevator.

As they made their way in, he shot her a playful smile. "So you don't like 'shorty,'" he observed. "I know you might be a little self-conscious about your height, so I get it," he teased, dimples stretching across his five o'clock shadow. "I apologize. I've been insensitive. So what should I call you?"

"How about Kirsten," she offered again. "Kirsten Beals."

He smiled wide. He seemed bent on getting to her. Boy, had he picked the wrong day. He gazed up at the elevator ceiling, his tall frame leaning comfortably against the wall. "How' bout 'butterfly'?"

She glared at him. Oh please... she thought as visions of Lisa, the yoga instructor, clouded her brain. More specifically, the butterfly tattoo on Lisa's shoulder. Ugh...

Her eyes practically rolled back into her head. She had to suck in another breath to keep from literally strangling him. "How about you just never address me at all," she suggested. "Like *ever.*"

He jerked his head to the side, a quick move she had noticed before which she found both charming and annoying. "Okay, so you don't like 'butterfly,'" he conceded as they exited the elevator.

Unfortunately, since he lived in the corner suite next to her mother's, she was stuck with him until she reached her door. So of course, she practically sprinted, walked as fast as her heels would allow.

"How 'bout 'dragonfly'?" he suggested, nipping at her heels. "I think that might suit you better."

As she reached her door and he made his way to his, he shot her a wink with that annoying twinkle in his baby blues. "Yep, that works...," he teased. "You're not a butterfly, you're a feisty little dragon."

She bit her lip. "Bye, Ethan."

A feisty little dragon?

She felt more like a pathetic tiny quivering mouse.

She slammed the door as she made her way inside. Her mother peeked out of the kitchen, an apple in her hand. If Lorraine was ever in the kitchen, it wasn't to cook. She was a modern day diva. And divas don't cook. Divas sustain themselves on fancy restaurants and their daughter's cooking, as was the case with Lorraine.

As soon as she saw her mother's face, Kirsten let the tears flow and lunged into Lorraine's arms. Lorraine held her tightly. Kirsten was so happy to have her mother. This wasn't just a scrape on the knee. It was much worse. As dramatic as Lorraine could often be, she really did love her daughter. Kirsten felt this love every day of her life. And she wanted this with her own daughter one day. She sobbed even harder when she realized this might not ever happen. The possibility of marriage, a white picket fence and babies seemed highly unlikely now.

Lorraine stroked her daughter's hair. "What happened?"

Gulping for air through thick sobs, Kirsten could barely answer her. "Lo-Logan..." she started, "he... he broke up with me."

Lorraine pulled away swiftly. "What?!" She gazed into her daughter's eyes. She didn't understand. It was incomprehensible.

Kirsten bit her bottom lip, not wanting to say the words. "He met someone else."

Lorraine's eyes grew wide. As a bestselling romance author, Lorraine usually had a way with words, but right then, she was at a complete loss for them. She had no idea what to say to her precious daughter. She just couldn't quite process the thought of Logan doing this. The boy seemed so sweet. How could he do this to Kirsten?

"I'm here," was all she could manage. She knew she had always been a little distant, too often caught up in her writing to give Kirsten the attention she deserved. She vowed to change that, especially now that her daughter really needed her. "Anything you want," she went on. "Shopping, mani-pedis?" Even as she said the words, she knew these things weren't her daughter's cup of tea. Her daughter was so different than her. She never quite understood it. Kirsten wasn't into all that posh girly stuff. For her, it had always been just about books. "I know it's not really your thing, but a day at the spa could do you good."

Kirsten smiled at her mother. She was trying so hard to make her feel better, and surprisingly it was working. Yes, perhaps a nice massage could be nice. And a little girl-talk with her mom over a latté. There was more to life than boys. After all, she still had her job, her health and her passions; reading and writing. She would follow her mother's lead, and just avoid talking about him, and thinking about him.

"Sounds good, Mom."

Lorraine shot her a playful smile, fine lines etched at the edges of her sparkling green eyes – even the Botox couldn't get to those. "Atta girl," she cheered with a bounce of her thick red curls.

"Like getting dumped wasn't bad enough," she told her mother. "Guess who I ran into at the elevators."

Lorraine smiled. "Your arch-nemesis," she ventured, "...the beautiful Ethan Fox."

Kirsten's eyes grew wide. "How did you know?"

"Just a hunch," she said. "You always get a certain look when you talk about him."

Kirsten frowned, thinking about the arrogant neighbor she just couldn't seem to shake. "A look of annoyance, you mean?"

"He's not so bad, Kirsten," she argued. "You're too hard on him. He's a nice young man."

Kirsten laughed out loud, and she didn't fail to notice the irony, and how odd it was that she would be laughing a mere hour after the most devastating break-up of her life. But her mother's comment had cracked her up because Lorraine was known for fancying younger men. She even currently had a handsome boy-toy. At thirty-five, Max was much younger than Lorraine, and only ten years older than Kirsten.

"Oh Mom," she said, still laughing. "We all know how you love young men," she couldn't help but say. But her laugh soon faded when she realized that at fifty-one, her mother's love life was much more exciting than her own would ever be. She had always wanted to be like her mother; charming, vivacious, and full of life. But she was the serious one. Someone had to be.

"Hell, life is short, Kirsten," Lorraine said, suddenly serious. "That's why I don't want you to dwell on this break-up... you need to move on."

Kirsten's heart sank again. "But Mom... five years."

Lorraine shook her head. "I don't care how many years you've wasted on that little scoundrel, but you're going to move on."

Kirsten nodded like a little girl being scolded.

"And to be completely honest with you," her mother went on. "I've always thought he was a bit too straight for you. I think you need someone more fun, someone who can add a little excitement to your life. Sometimes opposites attract, sweetie."

"So what are you suggesting, Mom?" Kirsten asked, slightly annoyed by her mother's antics. "That we go out clubbing, pick me up a rebound fling?"

Lorraine shook her head. "Oh no, no," she insisted. "It's too soon for another relationship. I was thinking you just need to have a little fun, try to live a little, act your age for a change."

"I'm perfectly fine living the way I live, Mother."

"I know, I know, Kirsten." She smiled sweetly at her, just the way she always did when she was up to something. "You just need someone to shake you up a bit, to bring you out of your shell... to loosen you up."

Kirsten sighed. "But you know I don't really have any friends." It was sad, but true. She had always been very introverted, and didn't need a lot of friends. But she would have liked at least one, a nice girl like herself she could confide in, and possibly occasionally gossip about her mother.

"No worries," Lorraine quipped. "I have just the right person for the job."

2

TEN FOR SUPER-HOT!

Kirsten squared her shoulders. "Hell, no."

Her mother shot her a playful look. "C'mon... he's really not so bad."

"Are you kidding me?" Kirsten scoffed. "He's the most pretentious man I've ever met. He struts around like he's God's gift to the world. I don't think he's ever addressed me by my name," she pressed on, determined to make her mother understand how much she despised the man, "even when I've repeatedly told him my name."

Lorraine laughed out loud. "That's just how Ethan is," she pointed out. "He doesn't address me by my name either. He likes to call me 'the beautiful Mrs. Beals,'" she added with a flip of her hair. "I kind of like it."

Kirsten rolled her eyes. God, even her mother was falling for this guy's tricks. But one thing was for sure – the smooth and sleek act wasn't working on Kirsten at all. Although she did not deny the fact that her dreams suggested otherwise.

"You're wired way too tight, Kirsten," Lorraine told her daughter. "He's just having fun with you. Just go with it."

Kirsten slouched back on her mother's smooth white leather sectional, staring up at the glittery chandelier above.

"This is exactly why I want you two to paint the town red," Lorraine went on, a glass of wine in her hand. Red wine had been deemed absolutely necessary for the occasion. It wasn't every day that your daughter got dumped. "Ethan is wild... he's fun... he could teach you a thing or two."

Kirsten smirked as a naughty thought flickered swiftly through her jumbled thoughts. Yes... she was sure he could. A guy like that could teach her more than a thing or two. She bit her lip to clear her head.

Jeez...

"Well, anyway, I've decided to invite him for dinner. This is my condo, after all," Lorraine pointed out with a tilt of her head. "And I can invite whom I wish to invite."

Kirsten shot her nose up. "Well, I can just make myself scarce."

Lorraine scowled at her daughter. "You will do no such thing," she insisted. "You will be here and you will make your famous Boeuf Bourguignon."

Kirsten sucked in a breath. She was a grown woman, free to make her own decisions. But she would never ever hear the end of it if she refused. Her Diva mother would sulk for days and give her the silent treatment. And she just did not have the patience for her mother's shenanigans.

She sighed as she conceded, "Fine..." she said, the word clipped. "But he's here for two hours tops. Any longer than that and I will physically kick him out myself."

Her mother laughed. "I highly doubt you'd be able to do that, sweetie. He's about twice your size."

HE STOOD AT THE DOOR, holding a bouquet of white roses, eyes gleaming. He wore his usual annoying smirk. "Hey, dragonfly."

He had said two words and had already managed to get her going. She smiled tightly at him, and took the flowers when he offered them.

"They're for your mother," he explained, "and you," he added with a little jerk of his head.

It was kind of sweet – the flowers. And he was dressed so nicely; a crisp white shirt and stylish slim-fit dark jeans. She had never seen him dressed casually before. He always sported the designer suits. Obviously he had made an effort. She couldn't quite look at him when she thanked him. "Please, come in."

He followed her to the living room and sat down on the white sectional. He smirked a little as he studied his surroundings. He seemed at odds with the ultra-feminine room. "This is kind of how I pictured the place."

Kirsten raised a brow, curious. "You've pictured our place?"

He shot her a wide grin. Kirsten looked away, knowing she had pictured his place too. She imagined it filled with sleek designer furniture. Lots of black leather. Weird modern art, and empty pizza boxes. A certain billowy headboard had also prominently featured in her steamy dreams. Truth be told, she was a little disappointed with herself. As much as she loathed the man, her petulant libido seemed bent on fighting her at every corner. "Um... would you like something to drink?" she asked, feeling one size too big in her own skin. God, what was taking her mother so long?

"I'll just have a water please," he said quietly as he studied her, all traces of his smirk gone. "Thanks."

She practically sprinted to the kitchen. "I'll get that for you right away."

She wanted to throttle her mother for putting her in this situation. She was introverted and never did quite as well as she would have liked in such social occasions. And especially when it came to tall, beautiful, arrogant men. She walked briskly to the living room and sat his drink down on the glass coffee table, not forgetting to place a coaster under the bottom of the glass. He smiled tightly at her and she scurried away awkwardly to her mother's room.

"What's taking you so long?" she asked her mother, the words a whisper. "You're being rude, Mom."

Lorraine smiled widely as she put on her dangling silver earrings. "All this doesn't happen as quickly as it used to, darling," she told her daughter, staring at her reflection. "A lady must always show her best self when a handsome gentleman comes calling."

"Oh please," Kirsten whined, tired of her mother's antics.

"Don't 'oh please' me Kirsten... you could have made a bigger effort," she pointed out. "What exactly is that furry shirt you're wearing?"

Kirsten looked down at her grey pencil skirt and short-sleeved pink fuzzy shirt. "What?... it's soft."

"Just because you're a librarian, Kirsten, doesn't mean you must always dress like one."

Kirsten followed her mother out of the bedroom, concluding that it was best not to take fashion advice from a fifty-one year old woman who wore flashy sequined purple tops.

Lorraine threw her arms out when she saw Ethan.

He stood to greet her. "If it isn't the beautiful Mrs. Beals."

'Oh please...' Kirsten thought, looking down at her silver watch. One hour and fifty-two minutes to go.

"Wow," Lorraine cheered. "Thank you so much for the beautiful roses," she offered as she bent down to smell them, her silicone-filled cleavage in full evidence.

Ethan sat back down on the sectional, his long legs looking at odds. "Thanks so much for having me."

"Oh," Lorraine said as she sat down next to him. "It's our pleasure. We'll have a grand time. Kirsten here, is quite the cook. She's making a delicious Boeuf Bourguignon."

Kirsten could feel the blush creep up her body. She smiled

shyly and wondered why she was suddenly behaving so strangely. "Uh... you're not vegetarian, are you?" she asked. He could have been. She had no clue.

"No, I'm a red-blooded American," he smirked. "I love a good steak."

"Well, you'll enjoy Kirsten's cooking then," Lorraine told him. "She's amazing."

His gaze lingered on Kirsten, his expression serious as he added, "I believe it."

Kirsten felt herself get weak at the knees. And she kind of wished she could kick herself straight.

Ethan dug into his meal with gusto. Mrs. Beals had been right. Kirsten was an amazing cook. How odd. She didn't seem like the type who would cook or eat much. She was such a tiny little thing. She was a quirky little thing too.

He noticed her the week he had moved into the loft building about a year before. She was carrying a huge pile of books. She was practically wobbling over. And when he offered to help, she scoffed. He introduced himself, waiting for her response. She simply nodded. And then came a small smile, here and there. But mostly it was looks of nonchalance. He didn't quite know what he'd ever done to her. He knew he came off strong with strangers but that was just him overcompensating. She wasn't giving him an inch. It had been hard getting to know her, practically impossible in fact. When Mrs. Beals extended an invitation to dinner, he jumped at the chance to break bread with his sister's favorite author. He even brought a copy of her latest hardcover for an autograph.

But he also wanted to get to know Kirsten too. The after-shave wasn't for the famous romance writer. It was for Kirsten. He didn't usually have to work hard to attract women. They flocked to him. A couple of drinks at his favorite spot and he'd be leaving with a gorgeous piece of ass. So why was he so intrigued in Kirsten's? It was looking perky and delicious, tucked in her little tight reasonable grey skirt. Thick framed glasses, conservative outfit, up-do. She was the complete opposite of the women he dated. Perhaps that was just it. He couldn't say he was attracted to Kirsten Beals, exactly. Or perhaps it was the chase he was after. He was like an animal in captivity. His prey usually came so easily to him. And Kirsten was absolutely off the menu. For one reason, she didn't seemed charmed by him at all. And for another, he was pretty certain she had a rather serious boyfriend, an uptight type he had seen her with. Maybe he was just looking for a challenge. Perhaps he was just bored.

"So, Ethan," Lorraine ventured. "How is business going?" She and Ethan were the ones carrying the conversation, idle chit-chat. Kirsten was mostly quiet, with a certain air of indifference. She truly did not seem to like him. This was new to him. Everyone liked him.

"It's been busy, as always," he replied with a quick glance in Kirsten's direction. She was twirling her fork around in her salad, acting like she was at a dreadfully boring work dinner.

It was time to stir things up.

"That's typical in the tech world. We're always coming up with new apps," he went on. "Right now we're working on this silly app where you can take a photo of someone and the app rates them on a scale of one to ten," he added with another glance in Kirsten's direction. She perked up. "Ten for super-hot."

Lorraine laughed softly. "Why, that does sound fun," she said with a playful grin. "I wonder how it would rate me."

"A ten," Ethan cheered. "For sure."

She laughed heartily. Ethan really liked Lorraine. She was so fun and young at heart. He was always chatting her up when he ran into her. It was hard to believe she and Kirsten were related. Kirsten seemed as uptight as they come. How he would love to loosen her up, he found himself thinking and shook his head. Damn, where was his mind?

"Very important work you folks are doing," Kirsten chimed in, finally giving them the courtesy of participating in their conversation. "You'll surely change the world in no time."

Her condescending tone got to him a little. It was time to play. "I suspect you wouldn't rate too well, shorty," he said with a smirk. "The app gives extra points for a um... a voluptuous chest."

Lorraine laughed out loud, throwing her head back. "I would get those extra points," she said. "But you're right, Kirsten would get a big fat zero in that department."

Kirsten glared at her mother and helped herself to some more red wine. She looked as if she needed it. He enjoyed getting to her. It was fun to see her fuming, her stuck-up air of decorum fading slowly.

"Sounds like a very classy app," Kirsten chirped.

"You'll have to excuse Kirsten," Lorraine offered. "She's feeling a little cranky. She's just been dumped."

Kirsten jerked toward her mom, slack-jawed and wide-eyed. "Mother!!"

"What?" Lorraine quipped. "It's the truth. There's no shame in it. The jerk dumped you cold after five years, to go run off with a yoga instructor."

Now, it all made sense to Ethan. Why Kirsten had been so pissy this past week. She had never been super friendly, but at least, she was usually civil. But today...

"I was telling her she should just get on with her life and forget all about him."

"Easier said than done," Ethan offered with another glance at Kirsten, who couldn't seem to look at him. "Break-ups are hard." Even as he uttered the words, he knew he was full of it. He had never been heartbroken because he had never cared. Casual sex was his life and he liked it that way.

"I was telling Kirsten," Lorraine went on, "that she should get out more... go clubbing, have a little fun."

Kirsten rolled her eyes and slouched back in her chair. Ethan enjoyed seeing her so disheveled. It was quite entertaining.

"But the problem is she doesn't really have any friends—"

"Mother!!"

"That's when I thought about having you over," Lorraine plowed on, completely ignoring her daughter's objections. "I thought you could show her the town, bring her out of her shell a little."

Ethan was taken aback. He hadn't expected this. Sure, he had been curious when Mrs. Beals had invited him for dinner. He was at a loss for words as he quickly glanced at Kirsten who was staring down at her skirt. Yes... his feisty little dragon wasn't so feisty after all. She looked more like a scared vulnerable little girl. He felt sorry for her. He decided to stop playing games. "I'd love to," he cheered. "I think that would be fun. I know a place I think you'd really like, Kirsten."

At the sound of her name, she raised her head slowly to meet his gaze. He was lost in her for a second or two. She had the most beautiful big brown eyes he'd ever seen.

It was the first time she heard her name on his lips. There was something very sexy about his voice, soft and low. And when he said her name, her heart had skipped a beat. And when she had looked up into his eyes, his gorgeous blue eyes were like a beautiful invitation, on ivory textured paper with golden edging, embossed scripted font and pretty ribbon. How could she say no?

The idea of painting the town red with Ethan sounded rather exciting. He may have been a little arrogant, but he sure seemed like the kind of guy you'd have a good time with – that, she couldn't deny. And perhaps, fun was just what the doctor ordered. It sure beat watching sappy romantic comedies and drowning herself in pints of ice cream. A little dancing might be a bit healthier.

She smiled shyly at him without a word. A night out or two. It wouldn't be the end of the world.

"We'll have fun," Ethan promised with a wide smile, turning to Lorraine.

"That's exactly what my little girl needs," Lorraine said. "A little fun. She needs to forget all about Logan."

"Logan..." Ethan said. "You two were serious?"

Kirsten tilted her head, not wanting to talk about Logan. "Yes... I thought he was going to ask me to marry him," she confessed. There was something about Ethan that made her suddenly want to tell him her whole story. There was a gentleness in his words and voice that was quite inviting. "But he dumped me instead."

Ethan winced a little. "I'm sorry."

"The worst part is..." she went on. She was on a roll. "I'll have to see him again in a few months," she told him, experiencing those old familiar feelings of dread at her core. "It's a fundraiser for the library we do every year and Logan's firm is highly involved. Logan is involved in many charitable organizations," she went on, remembering her ex. His charitable work had been one of the reasons she loved him, even when he often acted superior, belittling people who he deemed beneath him. "Anyway, it will be hosted by the library and since I'm in charge of all functions at the library, I need to be there. It's my job."

Ethan listened attentively. And she couldn't help but notice his beautiful hands has he traced circles around the bottom of his wine glass. She couldn't believe she was telling him all this. "And the worst part is," she went on. God, what was she doing? "He'll probably be there with his new girlfriend, Lisa, the hot yoga instructor... she has a tattoo and everything."

Ethan smiled. He couldn't help it. She was kind of cute, pouring her heart out like this. He didn't think she had it in her. It was nice to see there was a human being underneath the conservative skirt and fuzzy pink shirt. He loved her in that shirt. She looked so soft, like an adorable teddy bear he could just squeeze to death. He shook his head. "Yep... tattoos... they're not sexy at all," he said, trying to make her feel better.

She smiled. "Really?"

"Oh yeah... girls with high heels and tattoos. They're so over-rated," he told her with a wide grin. "I much prefer a nice buttoned up girl."

Both Lorraine and Kirsten laughed. Kirsten tilted her head a little and bit her bottom lip. The seductive gesture caught him completely off guard. He liked it. He liked it a lot. "And I bet you prefer granny panties over thongs too."

He laughed. "Of course, there's nothing like a good pair of granny panties... with little tiny flowers on them."

"I have a pair or two," she told him. "Maybe I could show you one day."

Lorraine was slack-jawed. She eyed her daughter with a mischievous grin. Ethan seemed amused. Perhaps there was a little bit of Lorraine in her daughter after all.

"I'd love to see that," Ethan offered with a playful grin. He was a pro at banter and innuendo. But for some reason, he was enjoying this a lot more than usual.

But Kirsten wasn't exactly as experienced at this as he was, and she soon faltered. "Uh..." she said a little awkwardly. "Were you guys ready for dessert?" She completely veered them off course and the flirting was officially done. "I have cookies."

"Sure," Ethan said, wanting to follow her to the kitchen and continue what they started.

She came back with a tray of shortbread and chocolate chip cookies. "Sorry," she said. "These are store-bought," she confessed as she set the plate on the table. "I love to cook but I don't bake much."

Ethan smiled. "That's funny. I don't cook but I love to bake."

"Really?" Kirsten ventured, wide-eyed.

"Yep... I make a mean apple pie," he gloated, helping himself to a shortbread cookie. "My nanny thought me... we would bake in the afternoon... muffins, pies, cookies... you name it. I loved it."

Kirsten smiled sweetly at him with a rather peculiar expression, as if she would have liked a little taste of not only his baking, but him too. "Sounds yummy."

Yep... he knew women enough to know she would love a little one-on-one time with him, perhaps continue the flirting they had barely started. "I could teach you, if you'd like."

He spotted the glint in her eye. "Uh..." She was speechless. He had clearly surprised her with the suggestion.

"Uh..." She soon recovered. "That sounds fun. I think I might like that."

Oh yes... she was up for it. "I'll teach you how to make a pie, from scratch."

She smiled. "Sounds great."

He was thrilled. He wasn't sure why. He'd always thought she was cute and interesting, but he had never quite seen her that way. But there was something about her... he wanted to help her. She had so much potential. There was a subdued sensuality about her, and it just needed to be released.

And he wanted to be the man to do that, the one to break her open.

3

—————

LET ME HAVE MY FUN WITH YOU

Kirsten wasn't sure how Ethan had managed to convince her to go to his place for a private pie baking lesson, but there she was, sporting a polka-dot apron and knocking at his door. She didn't want to admit to herself that she was quite excited at the prospect of seeing his apartment and spending some time with him. That sounded an awful lot like a crush.

And Ethan Fox was not the type she usually crushed on. She tended to fall for the boy-next-door, which ironically, he was. He was literally the man-next-door, but there was absolutely nothing boy-next-door-ish about him. He was a bad boy, a player, and she needed to constantly remind herself of that little fact. He was just playing her like he played everyone.

When Ethan opened the door, he shot her a playful smile. "Nice apron, dragonfly."

She smiled tightly and made her way in. His place was not too far off than what she had imagined, a sleek modern vibe with retro cool touches. As he welcomed her in the living room, she made a beeline for the red retro barber's chair. "Can I sit?"

He smiled at her. "Sure... it's comfortable."

"Where did you get this?" she asked, taking in the vintage movie posters covering the rustic brick walls, and all the retro 60s and 70s paraphernalia in bright hues of orange, blues, yellows and reds. It was like a kid's playroom. The energy filled her, made her happy.

"At an auction," he told her. "Cost me a pretty penny."

She leaned back into the chair, surprised by how comfortable it was. "I can imagine." As she stepped off, she noticed the view, practically a 360 degree view of the Seattle skyline, the tower and Elliot Bay. It was amazing and she could only imagine what it would be like at night. Being the corner unit, Ethan's loft had much better views than her mother's place. "Someone scored the corner piece with the extra icing."

He smiled bashfully, hands in the pockets of his faded designer jeans. "Yeah... I got lucky with this place. There were a lot of bids but I won out."

She didn't want to ask how much he had paid. Of course she wouldn't. She didn't care. She was just so amazed by the place. And when he led her to the ultra-modern gourmet kitchen, complete with double wide refrigerator, she was excited. The cook in her could only dream of the possibilities. She spotted the bright orange professional Kitchen-Aid mixer. "Wow, someone's a pretty serious baker."

He laughed, retrieving the ingredients needed for pie baking. "Ready to bake?" he asked, flashing his white smile, which matched the simple white t-shirt he wore. "Apple pie suit you?"

Kirsten loved a good apple pie. "Sounds great."

He inched in closer behind her. "Have you ever baked a pie before?" he asked, reaching over her for some mixing bowls.

She liked the proximity of him. He seemed like a different person today, without the pretentious suit. "No... it's all new to me."

He shot her a grin. "It's easy as pie," he joked.

She smiled, surprised by how well they were getting on. She

told herself to give him a chance. She realized that she might have judged him too soon.

He listed the ingredients as he poured them into the stainless steel bowl and started mixing. "You wait for the butter and flour to take shape before you add water," he instructed as he stirred. Then he proceeded to slowly add water. She cuddled up to him to take it all in. He smelled like vanilla... or perhaps that was the bottle sitting on the table. "Then, we need to knead the dough like this," he added as he demonstrated. She watched him eagerly, wanting to get her hands dirty too.

"Your turn," he said with a playful wink.

She sank her hands into the bowl, taking over. The sensation was new to her since she had never baked a pie before.

He watched her intently, leaning against the counter. "Work that dough, baby."

She laughed, enjoying the sensation of the dough on her hands. "Seems to be working."

"You're good with your hands," he teased.

She bit back a smile. "Oh... I am."

"I'm sure," he said and when she glanced in his direction, she spotted that glint in his gorgeous blues. Damn... he was good at this. He was a pro. He could get her worked up with a few innocent words and a playful stare. He made it look so easy.

And he hadn't even started. He stepped behind her and wrapped his arms around hers, his breath floating above her head, his hands covering her delicate fingers. "Let me help you."

As her heart skipped a beat or two, she panicked and faltered a little. "Uh... yeah..." she stammered as she swiftly made her way out of his hold. "You should probably take over." It was more than a little awkward, but then, Kirsten was used to being awkward, especially with gorgeous playful men.

He shot her a tight smile. "I'll get it ready for the fridge. It needs thirty minutes," he told her with a tilt of his head. "I thought we could talk."

Talk about what?

Kirsten washed her hands, suddenly regretting her decision to have undertaken *Pie Baking 101* with Ethan Fox. She dried her hands on her apron, making her way to the contemporary grey sectional sofa. She tilted her head as she studied the glass covered slab of tree he called a coffee table. There were tech magazines covering it, and she absent-mindedly flipped through one, thinking about Ethan. Why was he helping her? What was his agenda? Sex? She was sure there were easier roads to take to reach that end, especially when you were Seattle's most eligible bachelor.

He took a seat next to her, a little too close for comfort. And she suddenly got very nervous. Did *Pie Baking 101* include making out on the sofa while the dough refrigerated? Part of her wished it did, and the other part of her told her to rein in her misbehaved libido.

"So..." Ethan started, elbows propped casually on his leg. "You're probably wondering why you're here."

Kirsten sat up straighter, at a loss for words. "Um..."

"I'm sure you know it's not just about teaching you how to bake a pie," he went on, and her breath hitched. She had been right. He wanted to play a little. And she wanted to play too.

"The thing is," he finally managed. "I want to help you. I feel kind of sorry for you."

Her heart sank. His words cut. She didn't want his pity. As she stood to leave, he grabbed her hand. "Sit down," he ordered. "You need to hear this."

She didn't particularly liked to be bossed around, but he had her attention.

He held her hand as he fixed her, eyes intense. She was glued in place, under his stare. "I'm not a wise old man," he told her, "but one thing I do know, dragonfly... is women... and men. And how they relate... what men like," he carried on, eyes intense, "and what women like."

Her gaze was glued to his as she listened intently. Suddenly, she wanted to learn from the master.

"You're very beautiful, Kirsten," he said, his voice soft. The sound of her name on his tongue did crazy things to her. It was so easy for him. "You have a lot of potential and you just need to own it."

She looked down at her feet. He grabbed her chin and tilted her face to his. "Like right now," he said. "When a man tells you you're beautiful, you look him in the eye."

Speechless, she fixed him. God, he was stunning. The intensity in his gaze was unlike anything she had ever experienced. Pure sensuality. Her gaze traveled from his beautiful eyes to his full lips. She desperately wanted him to kiss her.

He let go of her face and smiled as he stood up, leaving her wanting. "You're what I like to call a 'fixer-upper,'" he told her with a smirk. "Lots of potential, but needs a little work."

She sat, slack-jawed. Apparently the arrogant Ethan Fox was there all along, momentarily taken over by this god of seduction. She stood to leave again. "No thanks. This shack is happy being a shack," she scoffed as she made her way to the door. "I don't need to be a pretentious fancy mansion." She didn't know if her words made any sense but she was trying to make a point. She had no desire to become his little pet project.

He nipped at her heels and grabbed her arm again. "Wait..."

She turned to him, livid. "I don't need your help, Ethan. I don't need your pity."

"I'm sorry," he offered. "I shouldn't have said... I just want to show that bastard of an ex-boyfriend of yours what he'll be missing."

At those words, Kirsten stood to attention. She wanted that too. She wanted to show Logan, show him how great she was. She wanted to make him see that he had made a colossal mistake and make him regret his decision, make him beg to get her back. Did she want to get back together with him? She didn't know. She just wanted to show him. "Okay," she conceded. "What's your plan?"

He smiled slowly, pulling her toward the sofa.

She grinned at him, a hint of a flirty smile. "Tell me all about it."

She tucked her feet under her legs as she settled onto the sofa, next to him. He crossed his long legs over the coffee table and leaned back beside her. "Well, first off," he started. "We need to get you a boob job."

Kirsten could not believe his words. The gall of him. She was halfway off of the couch when he grabbed her arm. "I'm kidding, dragonfly. I'm kidding."

She stared at his stupid grin and wanted to throttle him. "You better be."

He smiled. "Yep... I was kidding. I mean you don't have much to work with," he added, gesturing at her breasts. "But a nice push-up will do you fine."

She fixed him, open-mouthed. She would just have to learn to deal with his annoying ways, she reminded herself. It was a small price to pay for private lessons of seduction with the master.

"In terms of dressing, you don't need to go crazy," he carried on. "You will need to go a little sexier and tighter, but you don't want to go full-on tramp," he explained. "Men really don't like that. And the ones who do, you probably don't want... they'll just treat you like a whore, and expect you to be a porn star in bed."

Kirsten couldn't believe what he was telling her. "Oh... you are so wise, Mr. Fox." The flirty words weren't quite like her, but they had just slipped out. She was starting to warm up to him.

He smiled wide. "Of course I am," he said. "Now where was I?" he asked. "Oh yes..."

"So you're telling me you don't like the trampy girls."

He laughed. "Of course," he said. "Contrary to what you might think, dragonfly, I'm very discriminating when it comes to women. Only the best will do."

"Oh yes, of course." She sneered. "Then how come I see you with a different woman every weekend?"

He grinned again. "So you've been keeping tabs on me, dragonfly?"

She shook her head and tore her gaze away. "Not really."

"Well the thing is... there are a lot of beautiful classy women out there."

"I'm sure." Suddenly Kirsten hated the idea of him with other women. She realized this was ridiculous. They were just friends, after all.

"So makeup, hair and fashion," he went on. "My sister Meghan can help you with that. She's a fashion buyer, and as classy as they come."

Kirsten smiled. She didn't hate the idea of a little girly shopping time , a chance to remake herself, a whole new 'her' for a whole new life. She was moving on. "Should I lose the glasses?"

He bit his bottom lip as he stared at her for the longest time. She wondered what was going through his mind, and of course he didn't hesitate to tell her. "The glasses are kind of sexy," he said with a sinful grin. "You've got the whole 'sexy librarian' look, which is funny since you really are a librarian."

She rolled her eyes. She'd heard that one before.

"But maybe you can wear some contacts once in a while, like if you go clubbing or something," he suggested. "You have gorgeous eyes."

She smiled and stared at her feet again.

"Dragonfly," he scolded. "You're doing it again. Look at me when I tell you you're beautiful."

She jerked her head up, not wanting to get into further trouble with Mr. Fox. Although part of her kind of liked the scolding. Serious, slightly irked Ethan was wickedly sexy.

She tilted her head slightly and held his gaze. "Yes, Sir," she said slowly, the words floating off her tongue. As he fixed her without a word, his eyes darkened.

Ethan jerked his head away and stood from the couch in a hurry. "Um... you want something to drink while we wait?"

Damn, what is going on? Ethan wondered.

Suddenly little plain librarian from next door was making him hard. It was the way she had just looked at him. Those sinfully gorgeous brown eyes. Bedroom eyes. And suddenly his mind went to all sorts of crazy places: her naked body wrapped around him like ivy on a brownstone.

She wasn't even his type, or so he thought.

God... he suddenly wanted to teach her everything he knew. And then some. But she was so stand-offish with him. He wasn't sure if he could break through the ice-queen thing she seemed hell-bent on carrying on. But she was warmer than he thought. She was slowly melting under his stare. He had her, he knew it. He knew enough about women to know this, but for the first time ever, he really wanted to hold on to that, hold on to her. He didn't want to lose her by doing something stupid. And she was a prickly one. He kind of liked that about her. She wasn't throwing herself at him like all the others. He liked the chase, not quite knowing where he stood, the mystery.

He bit his lip, carefully measuring his words, which he never usually did. What was she doing to him? "I thought we could discuss our plan."

She nodded, attentive, those beautiful brown eyes fixed on him. She certainly wasn't making it easy to focus. He had over-seen hundreds of board meetings with the powerful; colleagues, investors, the richest of the rich. And somehow, he had never felt so out of his element. He didn't know where to start. He would have liked to start with just grabbing her by the rear and planting her right on top of him. But Kirsten wasn't the kind of girl who would take too well to that, or maybe she would. He didn't know. He didn't really know her. And he wanted to know everything. If there had been a *Kirsten Beals for Dummies,* he would have devoured every word, learned what made her tic. He decided that he would go over the steps of his plan in a business-like, formal way. He concluded she would appreciate his professionalism.

"I thought we could essentially focus on three things," he started. "The first being how you present yourself."

She glared at him for a second but didn't utter a word.

"What I mean is... you're beautiful. You just need to work with what you have," he added, flustered. "But we've talked about that already. Part two would be attitude," he carried on, "maintaining eye contact. It's all in the state of mind. If you think you're sexy, you will be. We won't be doing any official lessons. I mean, I don't have a guidebook to follow, but after a few hours with me... We'll play with flirting, dirty talk, sexting."

She laughed. "I don't sext," she told him, the words brimming with finality.

Damn, he was looking forward to that. The clever little thing would be so fun to play with. He was looking forward to pulling her out of her comfort zone. "You do now," he said casually.

She smiled at him. "And I dirty talk too?" she asked, not so much a question, but rather a tease. It seemed she was already on the right track. She would be a quick study.

"And we'll go on an official date," he went on. "Dinner and dancing, and you can show me your moves."

She laughed. "I don't have any moves."

"Oh, but you do." He smirked. "You do now."

"And then..." he carried on and faltered a bit. "If... if you're agreeable with this," he plowed on, feeling insanely nervous. He was walking a slippery rope and he didn't want to mess it all up. "We'll move on to sex, and I can teach you what I know... what men like."

She sat motionless, mouth open. He had done it. He had gone too far. Damn, he knew he shouldn't have added that last bit. But he was so damn horny. She was driving him crazy. And truth was, he couldn't wait to get her into his bed. He knew he could have gone about it in a more seamless way, a slow seduction, instead of this disastrous revelation. He should have never put it out there, in the plan.

Still, half a minute later, the poor thing was still speechless.

Kirsten was without words. She couldn't believe the man. Was he suggesting they have sexual intercourse so blatantly, like he was going over the day's agenda with his colleagues at work? Sex might have been something he did every day with countless nameless bimbos, but for her, it was more than that.

She cleared her throat. "Um... yes, quite the extensive plan you've cooked up."

He smiled. "I know it's not much... just at the top of my head, you know. But if you'd like something more substantial, I could make you an iPad presentation. We've got just the right app for that."

She shook her head and sat up straight. "I'm cool with the makeover and the date and the flirting," she told him, "but I think I'll take a pass on the sex."

She thought she saw a flicker of disappointment in his eyes but he recovered quickly. "As you wish," he said, standing swiftly. "But we'll have a good time, either way... I think our dough is ready."

He was obviously dismissing her because she wouldn't have sex with him. What a player. She didn't care. She had standards, after all.

Kirsten didn't fail to notice how his shoulders stretched against the fabric of his t-shirt as he scattered flour across the surface of the table. He shot her a quick wink as if he could read her thoughts. "The lesson officially starts," he declared as he pressed the dough against the hard surface, his fingers skilled. "Not the pie-making lesson," he clarified, "the mastery of seduction... we'll call it," he added with a soft laugh.

Kirsten smiled. She couldn't help it. He was being all kinds of hilarious. "Can I help?"

"Grab the roller," he instructed. "And I'll help you roll the dough."

As she wrapped her fingers around the handles of the roller and started rolling the dough, she felt a little uneasy. He stepped behind her and pressed his body against hers, too close. "Everything I do now is in the interest of your education," he whispered against her ear, his breath hot. Her heart skipped a beat, anticipating his next move.

"I want to see how you react, how you handle certain situations... my advances," he went on as his hands brushed hers, barely. As she rolled the dough, he traced a soft line on her arm with the tip of his finger, gently and slowly, from her wrist, along the length of her arm, all the way to the edge of her t-shirt sleeve. His touch felt amazing. He was giving her chills. She closed her eyes for a second, taking it all in, the wonderful smell of the dough, the soft feel of his touch.

"You're doing great," he added. "Just press a little harder." His fingers reached for a strand of her hair and he delicately pulled it back behind her shoulder, sending more shivers through her. He was literally making her body crazy. "Next time, wear a hair net."

"Um..." she said, flustered. She was so aroused, she could barely string a sentence together. "You're right... much... more sanitary."

He pressed closer against her and she felt his lips on her shoulder, his breath warm and all-consuming. God, he was turning her on. She couldn't take it anymore. She let go of the roller, and turned to him, her mouth reaching for his.

He fixed her with dark eyes. "Turn back around," he ordered.

And she did, very abruptly, wondering what the hell he wanted from her.

"Don't be so eager," he told her, "like you haven't had sex in ages."

I haven't, she thought but didn't utter a word.

He pressed his hands on her leggings-clad rear and pressed

his lips to the back of her neck. "Take your time. Let me seduce you," he mumbled against her skin.

She closed her eyes, wishing she were more patient. She so badly wanted to kiss him. Instead, she stood motionless like an idiot. He kept stroking her ass and her thighs, moving slowly down between her legs. Oh God...

She let out a soft moan.

"That's it," he told her. "I like that. Show me how great I make you feel. Communicate with me. Do you like this?"

She smiled as she closed her eyes. Yes, she could do this. "Yeah," she said, the word as smooth as honey. "I like that..." She felt rather than heard his soft chuckle.

"Now, talk a little dirty to me. Show me what you've got."

She stopped breathing for a beat or two, not knowing what to say... she was at a loss.

"If you don't get a little dirty with me, I'll stop touching you."

The ultimatum floated above her head, frustrating her. Damn him. She didn't want him to stop. "I... like that, baby." She didn't have to work at a seductive voice. She was so turned on, her arousal drenched every syllable. Breathless, she added in a whisper, "Touch me... feel how wet I am for you, baby." She felt his hand still for a beat, and he remained silent for the longest time.

Finally, he whispered against her ear. "Wow... you're a quick learner, dragonfly. You deserve a sticker."

She laughed. "Do you have any on you?" she asked. She wasn't thinking about stickers, but rather about condoms.

"N-no, I... I don't," he replied, his usually very even voice was now a complete mess. He was obviously as turned on as she was. "But... I'll do you better than a sticker, baby," he said as he reached between her legs. "I'm going to make you come."

She felt a rush a heat consume her core at his words. The thin fabric of her leggings barely created a barrier between his skilled fingers and her pussy. She closed her eyes and stood on the tip of her toes as she propped her ass up and spread her legs giving him full access. He pressed his fingers against her hard, back and forth. She couldn't believe she was about to get off standing over pie dough.

"Now, don't turn around," he told as he kept pleasuring her. "Just reach out behind you, and touch me too."

She reached for him and felt him through the thick fabric of his jeans. He was so hard... and so big. She turned to him, wanting to kiss him.

He held her back. "No, turn around," he growled. "I want to bend you over the table and make you moan," he told her as he pressed his hand on her back. "Let me have my fun with you and just enjoy it."

She let herself go. As ridiculous as she felt in her silly polka dot apron, she melted into his hand as he rubbed her senseless. Her climax came on quickly, slowly spreading heat through her and making her cry out loud in pleasure, the sound of her orgasmic moans echoing off the walls. God, he could make her feel so good. She had never been happier to be a woman than she was at that moment, to be able to enjoy someone's touch this intensely. She had forgotten what that felt like. She could only imagine what he could do to her, naked.

When she came to, she was slightly mortified. "You can turn around now," she heard him say. But she didn't want to. She didn't want to face him. She slowly reluctantly turned to him.

She couldn't quite look at him as she studied the tiny flowers on her socks. He took her chin in his hand, just as he done before and held her face to his. "Look at me, dragonfly... tell me you loved that."

She smiled and looked straight into his beautiful eyes, the color of a tropical sky. "I loved that."

"That was amazing... seeing you come apart like that, lose all your inhibitions under my touch. It's good for a man's ego."

She pressed her hand against him and felt him still hard as a rock. "I want to touch you too."

4

I BELIEVE YOU GET AN A+, MISS BEALS

God... had he wanted to kiss her. But this wasn't about getting into a relationship, about starting something he couldn't finish. He didn't want to give her the wrong idea. Because if there was one thing he knew about Kirsten Beals is that she was definitely the type who got emotionally involved. He'd have to thread carefully with her. But all he wanted to do when she had turned around and fixed him with those beautiful eyes full of desire, was to bite that delicious bottom lip of hers.

He hadn't planned to do what he had just done. It hadn't been part of the 'lesson'. He had just had the sudden urge to make her scream in pleasure, to see her lose her inhibitions under his spell. And she didn't disappoint. Seeing the ordinarily very proper and put-together woman completely lose herself under his touch, under his control, was so amazing. He couldn't get enough of her. He wanted to please her all over again.

And now... she wanted to pleasure him too. As much as he wanted that, this wasn't about him. It was about her. And a nice cold shower in the near-future would have to do. As she pressed her hand on him, he almost lost his resolve. He was still so hard and her hand would feel so good, but they weren't quite there yet.

They were moving too fast. And they needed to take things slower. He grabbed her hand reluctantly and stopped her. "Let's keep the lesson on manual pleasuring until a bit later."

She eyed him with a surprised expression. "Are you sure?"

He smiled at her. No, he wasn't sure. He wanted her hands all over him. "When you jerk off a guy, it should come naturally. It shouldn't involve a conversation," he pointed out and turned his back to her. He needed to get away from her to stay on the right track. Suddenly he was veering off into emotional attachment territory, a place he had never ventured before. But with her, it was different. There was something so lovable about her. He didn't want to ever let go of her. Ever.

"What I need you to do is to peel some apples for me," he said as he handed her a bowl of Red Delicious apples and a peeler. She started peeling without a word, confusion and hurt written all over her face. The poor girl couldn't quite seem to keep up with him. There was obviously a lot more work to be done.

Kirsten had no clue what was going on. One minute, they were making a pie, and the next he was draped over her, rubbing her into ecstasy. It was amazing, until he got all weird about it. And now she just wanted to crawl out of her skin. They peeled and chopped apples, added some spices, put the pie together, complete with a lattice top. That part had been fun, and she had almost forgotten all about their earlier sexcapade. They did all this under a very disquieting silence. When he pronounced the pie done and slipped it into the oven, she thanked him. And as she closed the door behind her as she left his place, she could finally breathe properly.

~

LATER THAT NIGHT, over a cup of tea, her mother asked her how the pie baking went. Thankfully, Lorraine was reading the paper and didn't notice Kirsten's face turn crimson red.

"Uh... it... it was great," Kirsten told her, remembering the sensations Ethan had brought out in her. She hadn't realized her body had so many nerve endings until that moment. "Baking an apple pie is a really long process actually," she added casually. Especially when one takes an intermission for a little sexual play, she thought with a smile.

"That's why I've never made one," Lorraine added, her head still buried in her paper.

"It's fun," Kirsten told her. And she blushed again, thinking about Ethan' arms wrapped all over her. It was all she could think about.

Her cell chirped. It didn't chirp often since her break-up with Logan, and she was glad for the distraction, wondering who it could be. Her breath hitched when she saw Ethan's name.

Hey ;)

Hey ;), she replied.

Not exactly original, she knew, but she wasn't quite sure what else to say. Her heart was beating so hard, probably stealing the oxygen from her brain.

Where r u? What r u doing?

Am in the kitchen, having tea with my mom.

—

No, no, no... you are not.

But I am.

No... you r in bed. Always say u r in bed.

She almost laughed out loud, realizing what he was doing. This was all part of the lesson. Well, she was game.

I am in bed. Naked.

;)... that's more like it.

I was thinking about u. About what u did to me.

She waited a while for his reply, wondering where he was.

I LOVED doing that to you.

She bit her lip as she read the message, suddenly aroused. She wanted to play.

I want u to do that again. Soon. And I want to do it to u too.

Yeah baby, me too. You were beautiful.

Suddenly, she wanted him... now. She could barely contain herself.

Where r u? What r u doing?, she typed, hoping he was right next door.

At a club with some buddies.

Her heart sank. He was just having a little fun with her, most likely while waiting at the bar for his drink order. He would undoubtedly be leaving with a tall gorgeous bimbo in no time. If she stood against the front door and looked out the peep hole, she could probably see them walk by. Of course, she would never do that, but the fact that the thought had even entered her mind disturbed her a little.

Having a lot of fun, no doubt, she wrote, shoulders sagging.

I am surrounded by beautiful women, and all I can think about is you.

What a bunch of crock, she thought. She had had just about enough of Mr. Smooth.

Bye Ethan.

What?! That it?

Bye

You have failed miserably at sexting... I give you a D-.

D-? I will take it. Sounds good to me. Now leave me the fuck alone.

She wasn't quite sure why she was suddenly so angry and vulgar. But she knew it had a little something to do with jealousy. She hated that he was out there, 'surrounded by beautiful women', as he put it.

Grade revised. I give you a B- for the use of the word 'fuck', although the context is all wrong.

She couldn't help but laugh. Suddenly, she wanted an A+ and she knew she had it in her. Her fingers trembled as she typed the message, going as fast as she could, not wanting to lose her nerve.

**Ethan... get those bimbos off u, and come here and fuck me. All
I can think about is u between my legs.**

I will be there in five!!!

Oh God... Was he serious? Her heart was pounding hard
against her rib cage. She hadn't expected this. Here she was doing
the Jumble and having tea with her mother, and suddenly she
was about to be fucked senseless. She was absolutely not wearing
the right kind of underwear. She raced to her room. Her phone
chirped again and she lunged for it.

I was kidding. U get an A+. That was hot!!!

Her heart sank. He was playing with her.
Asshole.
She was driving him insane. When he read those words, his
dick had gone from 0 to 60 in about two seconds. He wasn't sure
if she was serious or not. She couldn't be... she was having tea
with her mother for heaven's sake. She couldn't have been serious. And besides, he didn't want to go there quite yet. He didn't
want to get too involved with her. He would be better off going
home with one of the gorgeous women at the club. But the
problem was he didn't want any of them. All he wanted was
Kirsten. She was all he could think about. He hadn't been lying
when he had written those words.

HERE HE WAS, acting like a complete lost cause again, going over
to the Beals under the pretext of being neighborly and bringing
freshly baked goods. But he knew he was so full of it. He knew
what he really wanted was to see Kirsten again. That little text
conversation between the two of them had worked him up good.

Sure, he'd sexted women before, much filthier stuff, much longer conversations. But none of them had managed to arouse him as much as Kirsten did. He was tossing and turning all night, thinking about her. She was the first thought he had when he woke up.

So now he was standing at her door with the pie they had baked.

Lorraine answered with a big smile. He could see the resemblance between Kirsten and her mother when they smiled. They both had that wide infectious down-to-earth grin.

"Ethan," she cheered. "You brought pie."

He handed her the plate. "Yeah, it's the one Kirsten and I baked." A vision of Kirsten brought to orgasm suddenly clouded his brain. He shook it off instantly. He wondered if he could think straight for even a single second. It seemed like he hadn't ever since that Beef Bourguignon dinner.

He smiled when he spotted Kirsten in her flannel pajama pants and pink tank top. How he would love to rip those off of her, he mused. Damn, there he went again, fixated on sex... sex with her specifically. She folded her arms over her breasts but not before he spotted the outlines of her nipples. Damn. He had to focus not to get aroused again.

"Hi," she said, shy. "Thanks for the pie."

"I thought you'd want to taste your first masterpiece."

"Are you sure you don't want any," she asked. "I can save you a slice."

Here was the perfect excuse to get her at his place again, but he couldn't go there. He knew if he had her at his place, he would certainly have his way with her. And she would most definitely let him. But Kirsten wasn't the kind of girl you played with like that. She was too serious. He cared for her and he didn't want to hurt her. He was a player, not boyfriend material. "No," he smiled as he told her, "I can make another one if the craving strikes... easy as pie."

She smiled and thanked him again, one arm still bashfully crossed over her chest. She did not invite him to stay. He understood. After all, it was early morning and she was still in her pajamas, probably about to get ready for work.

All future meetings would have to be conducted in public locales, he concluded. He played the possibilities in his head as he walked to work. Cafés, restaurants, coffee shops, public parks. It would be for the best. And he was starting to rethink the last lesson: sex. It would probably be best if he just went over the basics without a hands-on lesson. His insane attraction to her had made him suggest it at first, but now that he had gotten to know her better, he realized what a horrible idea that would be with a woman like Kirsten.

As much as he wanted to, he couldn't do that to her. Because if there was one thing he was not interested in, it was the whole relationship and marriage thing. Why fall in love and marry a woman, and father a few kids, if she's just going to leave you for the first tattooed brooding artist she sees. He was not walking in his father's footsteps. He had inherited his smarts for business, but not his soft heart. He could still remember, after all these years, the pain his father had suffered at his mother's hands.

Kirsten sat at the fountain at the shopping center, pulling at the sleeves of her sweater, surprised at how nervous she was to be meeting Meghan. Ethan had told her Meghan was great, and very down-to-earth. But still... Kirsten hated first impressions.

She knew it was her as soon as she spotted her in the distance; tall heels, blow-out, gorgeous sheath dress and matching jacket. The girl definitely had style.

Meghan practically sprinted in her heels. "You must be Kirsten."

Kirsten wondered for a second how she could be so sure. "Yep, that's me," she offered with a smile.

"I knew because Ethan told me all about you."

Kirsten wondered what he had told her. Probably something along the lines of 'look for a short uptight nerdy girl with geeky glasses'. Or perhaps it was something a little more flattering. She didn't dare ask. "It's nice to meet you," she said instead, following her new girlfriend's lead as she tilted her head and suggested getting started. This woman did not waste any time, and Kirsten liked that.

They practically raced from store to store, picking up makeup, lingerie (which Kirsten hoped she would get to use sometime in the near future, perhaps with Ethan), and a few token pieces for work and play (conservative but slightly seductive). Meghan was really a pro, moving along with the efficiency of someone who had clearly done this many times before. Kirsten was delighted. She usually hated shopping and often had no clue where to go. They followed up with a sushi lunch at the food court.

"Thanks so much, Meghan," Kirsten offered over a tray of California rolls, her favorite. "It's so nice of you to take time out like this to help me. I'm pretty useless when it comes to shopping and fashion."

Meghan smiled wide and Kirsten couldn't help but notice how much she looked like her brother, same engaging blue eyes and wide smile. "Are you kidding me," she cheered. "Shopping is what I live for. And when Ethan told me all about you, I couldn't wait to help him with his little project."

Kirsten sneered. "He called me his little project?"

Meghan laughed. "He did. But he said it with the best of intentions. He sounds like he's really into it. I haven't seen him this animated in a while," she added just before popping a sushi roll in her mouth.

Kirsten smiled. She liked the idea of Ethan being excited about her, even if it was just about achieving a goal, seeing it through to its fruition. He seemed like the goal-oriented type. His success would certainly indicate as much. She wanted to learn more about the enigmatic Ethan Fox and this was the perfect opportunity to do so. "So you two are close?"

Meghan nodded with gusto. "Thick as thieves. We're best friends."

"That's nice." Kirsten wished she had a sibling too. She always had. She had always vowed that when she had children, she'd have at least two.

"He's only two years older than me. We were always close," Meghan carried on. "But we got even closer when our parents divorced."

"Oh... I'm sorry," Kirsten offered. "My parents divorced too... well they separated. They were never married," she trailed off, hating how awkward she always got in intimate conversations.

"So you must know how it is," Meghan went on. "Our mother left our dad for an artist, and left us with a succession of nannies. We'd see her once in a while when the mood struck her," she carried on, sipping her iced tea, having abandoned her food. "And to make matters worse, shortly thereafter, our father paraded around with a bunch of gold-diggers."

"Wow," was all Kirsten could say. "And I thought my childhood was interesting."

Meghan smiled wide. "I can't believe your mother is Lorraine Beals... she's my favorite. It must have been so much fun growing up with her."

Kirsten gave her a tight smile. "It was and it wasn't. My mom was always really into her writing so I kind of took to cuddling next to her on the sofa. And while she tapped away on her laptop, I read books."

"Oh... that's so cute."

Kirsten liked Meghan. She'd always been quick to decide whether she liked a person or not, as she had with Ethan. He had gotten a 'no' at first impression. But his sister got a definite 'yes'.

"So after lunch, we'll head off to this little place I know for a cute cocktail dress. Every single girl needs a sexy little dress."

"Sure," Kirsten agreed. She owned a few dresses but none she could have described as 'sexy little dress'.

"And then we'll go back to your place and I'll give you a quick makeover, teach you a few tips."

Kirsten smiled and gestured to herself. "Yeah... I probably need it. This is as good as I get when it comes to makeup and hair."

Meghan drained her glass of iced tea. "You look nice," she told her. "You just need a little more for nighttime, for going out. You have such gorgeous eyes. We could really make them pop."

And hour later, they were at the cashier buying a beautiful yellow designer cocktail dress. Meghan had gotten a discount of 20%. It was a little more than Kirsten usually paid for a dress but she thought it was about time she invested a little in herself. She had really liked the dress. The color suited her coloring and the fabric was so luxurious. It made her feel like a princess, a naughty sexy princess.

"God, I wish I had your hair," Meghan said as she curled the last strand of Kirsten's long dark mane. "You are so lucky."

"But you have great hair," Kirsten argued. "Do you have any idea how many women would kill to have naturally blonde hair."

"Yeah... but it's thin," Meghan explained with a little tease at Kirsten's crown. "Yours is luscious and thick, something a man could really sink his hands into."

At Meghan's words, Kirsten imagined Ethan's long fingers in her hair. She shook her head clear.

"You don't like it?"

Kirsten smiled. "No, I love it." She stood and added one last dab of lip gloss, a final touch-up. She looked completely different.

She was still the same woman, but more confident, sexier. She loved it.

A mischievous grin slowly stretched Meghan's lips. "Now, let's go show you off to my big brother, and see what he thinks of all my hard work."

Kirsten's heart skipped a beat at Meghan's words. She was both scared and excited. What would Ethan think?

As Meghan tapped the door, she smiled wide at Kirsten, a silent encouragement of sorts. Ethan answered and swallowed his little sister in his arms with a bear hug. He paid no attention to Kirsten. Only because... he hadn't noticed her.

But when his gaze fell on her, he faltered for a second and took her in with wide eyes, from top to bottom, and back up again. "Wow."

She blushed. And she couldn't believe she was blushing. She wished she could say something clever instead of standing there like a statue, turning crimson under his stare. But it was no use. Her brain was simply not functional under his scrutiny. She wanted his approval. After all, this was all part of the lesson.

"So what do you think?" Meghan ventured.

He bit down a playful smile. "I like it. I believe you get an A+, Miss Beals."

5

SO MR. FOX APPROVES?

Kirsten held her breath. God... he was being so seductive. He didn't seem to care that his sister was standing right there.

Almost as if following his cue, Meghan walked towards the door. "Well, I should get going. I'm late meeting Kyle."

"Sure," Ethan said, not taking his eyes off Kirsten. Suddenly, he couldn't have cared less about his little sister.

Kirsten was feeling all out of sorts. She did not have the experience to handle the look he was giving her. She definitely needed more lessons. "Yeah, I should go too," she said, following Meghan back to the door.

He rushed to her and grabbed her wrist. "Wait..." he said. "We need to discuss this dress."

Meghan shot Kirsten a mischievous smile. She too, knew what her brother was up to. "Have fun, guys," she cheered as she left.

Oh my... the way Ethan was staring at her was intense.

"About this dress," he started, delicately wrapping his arm around her waist. He was putting her on the spot again. Was this part of the lesson? Or was this just about him wanting her? She didn't know how to react. She decided to play it cool, to not get too excited, like she had the last time he had seduced her. Perhaps he was testing her.

Looking at him straight in the eye and acting coy, she asked, "What about it?" She was learning. Slowly but surely.

"It's sexy as hell," he told her, playing with the hem of the fabric, rubbing it between his fingers, "and soft."

She smiled. "I know. That's what I like about it too," she told him." "So Mr. Fox approves?"

He pressed her closer against him. "Very much." His gaze fixed hers for an eternity before he spoke again. "You look beautiful."

She was at a loss for words. His sweetness was unexpected. He took her hand and she walked with him in the tall heels she had chosen just for the dress. As he sat on the edge of the back of the sectional sofa, he pulled her close to him. She was sure he was going to kiss her, but instead he just tucked a strand of hair behind her ear. "My sister did an amazing job," he told her, baby-blues intense. "You look very... fuckable."

She felt a rush of heat between her legs at the words on his lips. That's just what she wanted to be at this moment. Fuckable. She wanted him to have his way with her. But then he pushed her away softly and asked her to turn around. And she did.

He trailed his finger along the embroidered edge of the deep V cut. "I love the back."

She closed her eyes, enjoying his touch and wanting more. "Take it off," she whispered, the words barely audible.

His breath was warm on her shoulder as his hand stilled. "Pardon... what was that?"

"Take off the dress," she repeated, a little louder.

"I can," he said, his voice soft. "And what then... what do you want then?"

She couldn't say the words.

"Tell me what you want," he pressed, the palm of his hand hot on her back. "I want to hear you say it."

"You..." she started, gathering the courage to say what was on her mind. "You said I looked fuckable," she added, her voice shaky. Her heart pounded as she struggled to find the courage to say the words out loud. This behavior wasn't like her, but then again, Ethan had a way of completely consuming her, like a drug, making her behave completely unlike herself.

"Then fuck me," she finally whispered the words, and as she did, an intense pressure consumed her entire core. She desperately needed it to be released. "That's... what I want," she added, breathless.

The words had barely slipped out of her mouth when he pressed himself against her and slammed her against the back of the sofa, one hand clawing at her back zipper and the other pulling at her hair. She realized how intense he was as his mouth bit at the flesh on the back of her neck. She was his. Completely his. Her body had completely melted under his touch. He trailed his tongue down her back as he unzipped her. She still couldn't believe they were doing this as he peeled the dress off.

She knew this was just a rebound fling. She told herself this didn't mean anything. He kissed the soft flesh of her rear as he peeled off her pink cotton panties, and she literally ached for him. She wanted to turn around to kiss him, but she remembered the previous lesson when he had told her not to be so eager. And obviously, this boy had a little bit of an ass fetish. She reveled in him, and with every touch, every lick and bite, she got more aroused. And then suddenly, as he slid her panties around the tall sexy heels, reality set in.

"Ethan..." she breathed. "Do you have a..."

He pulled away. "Not on me... but just a second. Do not move an inch."

He raced to his desk. She closed her eyes, anticipating his return. She felt absolutely wicked leaning against the sofa in nothing but her sexy heels and brassiere. He was quick but it still wasn't quick enough. She couldn't wait to have him inside her.

He trailed kisses down her back as he stroked her ass. "How much do you want me?" he asked and she could feel his smile pressed against her shoulder.

She closed her eyes trying to lock in the feel of his touch, the sound of his voice, his earthy smell. "So much..." she breathed.

He trailed his fingers to her wetness and they both knew there was no more foreplay needed. He was gentle when he sank into her. He felt so fantastic. She couldn't believe how good he felt. It had been way too long.

"You feel amazing," he breathed.

She let out a languid moan as he pushed deeper. Her eyes practically rolled back into her head as he pressed harder into her, hitting her sweet spot. He grabbed her hair at the nape as he brought her closer and closer with every thrust. He pulled it, and she liked the wildness of that, the fact that he was a little rough with her. The mild pain incurred blended deliciously with her pleasure and only aroused her more. He was so passionate. Logan had never fucked her quite like this. She closed her eyes as the sensations took over her entire core, and reached the best climax of her life. His followed right behind, the sound of it echoing off the walls. It aroused her to hear the sounds of his pleasure, pleasure her own body was giving him.

When they had both fully recovered, she could suddenly see more clearly. What was she doing, draped over his sectional, nude, like a trollop? Sweet heavens, she had let him bring her to orgasm over a table, and take her from behind over the back of a sofa. And she hadn't even kissed him yet, hadn't even seen him naked yet.

What was he doing to her? She had always been a good girl, a missionary, in bed, with the lights dimmed kind of girl. This bad boy was turning her into a bad girl.

And she had to admit to herself... she absolutely loved every second of it.

Damn. He just had no control when it came to her. He had

not wanted to have sex with her so suddenly, so early on. He had not wanted to get a taste. Because now that he had, he wanted her all over again. He would have to rein himself in, control his impulses. He was not going to let that happen again. It was a one-time thing. He had wanted to kiss her so badly when she looked at him with those beautiful eyes of hers, and he had been able to talk himself down, because he knew that if they kissed, they would both want more.

He had pushed her away. But then, he absolutely lost it when she said she wanted to be fucked, so blatantly. So sweet, she was, standing there in her pretty yellow dress, yet so damn bad too. He had just lost his marbles. And when he had gotten that dress and those panties off, and had seen her precious behind, he was done for. She had the sweetest little ass he'd ever seen.

Just a minor setback, he told himself. No harm done. They both thoroughly enjoyed themselves, after all. The pleasures of the flesh... that's all it was. Now, it was time to buck up. Teach her a thing or two. And then set her on her way.

As Ethan helped her zip her dress back up, she could sense that something was wrong. He had gotten all serious and distant. And this hurt her a bit. Was this how he treated all the women he had sex with? Suddenly she felt used. But then again, she had used him too. It was a mutual arrangement as far as she under-stood. He was probably concerned she'd fall madly in love with him just because he had sex with her. She wasn't stupid. She knew this didn't mean anything to him. He was a notorious player and what they had just done had most definitely been just sex. It was in no way love-making. They hadn't even kissed.

She smoothed down her hair and smiled at him. "Don't worry, Ethan," she said matter-of-factly. "I know how this works. Just two people having sex... getting off. I'm not going to run off and plan our wedding." She knew she was being a little crude but that's exactly what she was going for. Nonchalance.

He shot her a tight smile. "I didn't mean to let that happen."

"Then why did you?" She wanted to hear him say how much he had wanted her. She couldn't get enough of his desire.

"You can't stand in front of me, looking like that, and ask me to fuck you, and expect me not to do it, Kirsten. I'm a guy."

"So, how did I do?" she asked with a grin. "I thought we weren't getting to that lesson for a while."

"We weren't supposed to," he told her. "And now that's it's done, we should probably not do that again."

She laughed. "But you didn't really teach me anything."

He smirked. "I'm not sure there's anything to teach. You seem to have it down pat," he pointed out, remembering the way she had been... so wanton. It was hard to reconcile the uptight proper librarian with the wild woman he had just been with. And she seemed eager for another lesson.

"Perhaps we could attempt a more in-depth lesson, next time, and go over the particulars. That one was pretty quick," she pointed out playfully.

He laughed. "Are you saying I was a quick draw?"

"Well, you certainly didn't waste any time."

He shook his head. "Well, look at you. Can you blame me?"

She liked driving him wild. She liked him when he was playful like this. She inched her way closer to him, her heels clicking against the hard wood floor. "But seriously," she said, her gaze glued to his. "You didn't teach me how to undress you, how to touch you, how to please you." A whisper of a smile curved her lips as she saw the flicker of desire in his eyes and realized she had a certain power over the gorgeous Ethan Fox. He was just a man, after all.

He drew in a breath. "I can imagine you're pretty good at that already."

"I am," she said and shot him a wicked smile as she headed towards the door.

When Kirsten did her very short 'walk of shame' back home (just a few steps), she couldn't help but smile. That had not gone as she expected. She had anticipated Ethan might like the sight of her all gussied-up in a dress, but she never in her wildest dreams, imagined he would completely lose himself and so utterly have his way with her.

As she tip-toed quietly to her room, her mother scared the hell out of her. "Kirsten," she exclaimed. "Why, look at you. You look gorgeous."

Kirsten was on edge. She knew her mother could read her like a book. "Yeah... my friend Meghan gave me a makeover."

Lorraine eyed her from top to bottom. "Well, the girl certainly knows what she's doing. Where'd you meet her?"

"Uh..." Kirsten hesitated, certain her mother could see that her daughter had just had the most amazing sex of her life. "She's Ethan's sister."

Lorraine smiled wide, finally cluing in. "I see," she teased. "Are you coming back from Ethan's?"

There was no sense hiding it. Kirsten could feel the blush spread across her cheeks. "Y-yes..."

"Oh my..." Lorraine whispered, hand to mouth. "You two are..."

"Mom," Kirsten objected. "I really don't want to discuss it."

"But... my dear," Lorraine said, pulling her daughter by the hand as she dragged her to the white sofa. "It must absolutely be discussed."

"Why, Mom?" Kirsten whined. "Why must it be discussed? This is so inappropriate."

Lorraine laughed. "I don't want to hear all the juicy details... I'm not your best girlfriend," she conceded. "I just think we should discuss Ethan."

Kirsten perked up. "What's to discuss?"

Lorraine shot her a tight smile. "I know you, Kirsten. And I know Ethan... or his type, at least," she started softly. "What I'm saying is I'm glad you're having a good time. That's what I wanted for you. You're young, you're pretty... that's exactly what you should be doing."

Kirsten smiled. "So what's your point, Mom?"

"You just need to be a bit careful... guys like Ethan," she faltered a little, searching for words. "What I'm trying to say is this is not one of my romance novels, sweetie," she went on, holding her daughter's hand. "Ethan is the kind of guy who's out for fun. Don't take him too seriously. Don't let him break your heart. Don't think about him as 'the one', just the 'fun for now' guy."

Kirsten sat up straight. She didn't like this conversation at all. "So you're saying just enjoy fooling around and don't get all hearts and flowers about it."

Lorraine beamed. "Yes, exactly."

Kirsten was officially sick and tired of this sweet little image she projected. Even her own mother felt sorry for her. "Well, you'll be glad to know... so far, we've done it on a table and on the back of a sofa, and I haven't even kissed him yet."

Lorraine's mouth fell open. "Well, you seem to have the hang of it. I suppose this conversation is pointless."

Kirsten stood suddenly, her mouth a hard line. "Yes, it is."

She scurried to her room, upset. Why couldn't her mother not mind her own damn business for a change? She had everything under control. She was very well aware of everything that Ethan was and was not. She certainly didn't need it drilled into her head.

She was in full control of her emotions. She could handle this. Just fine.

THAT WOMAN WOULD BE the end of him. Ethan needed a distraction now. But for the first time in a long time, he didn't crave the distraction of random women. All he could think about was her. He threw himself into his work to keep his thoughts at bay. He worked out more than ever to ease the tension. And he relied on his other vice to distract himself. This was nothing a game of Grand Theft Auto or Mortal Kombat couldn't fix.

Kirsten couldn't quite focus. Images of Ethan clouding her brain constantly: Ethan peeling off her dress, shoving her against the sectional, pleasuring her over pie dough. Such inappropriate thoughts to be having in a library. Focus was a large part of her job. With overseeing everything from circulation, special events, readings, and classes, she had her plate full and she had to be productive every day, no time for dilly-dallying. In fact, she prided herself on her productivity. But the last few days had been hard, the hours getting away from her. She didn't have enough time to check off the things she needed to do. Even her manager had noticed and had made a comment or two.

Kirsten really needed to get her act together today, but how could she do that when all she could think about was the upcoming 'big date' she and Ethan had planned. It was part two of the lesson. He had told her he would be giving her tips on dating, since she had very little experience in that department. She would definitely be a fish out of water. She had only dated two boys in her life. Her first, Mark, had been a high-school sweetheart and there really had been no dating at all with him. And then, she had met Logan at a fundraiser at the library and there had only been one or two dates before they were an official couple. She couldn't help but wonder how a woman was supposed to carry herself on a date these days. She was hoping Ethan would offer some priceless knowledge. Lord knew, he sure had gone on plenty of dates. He had a wealth of experience.

KIRSTEN WAS nervous as she waited for Ethan. She tugged at her frilly skirt as she paced back and forth in her mother's condo. He only lived a few steps away. She wondered what could be taking him so long. They had agreed that he would pick her up at 3:00

PM sharp. They were going to Kubota Gardens for a leisurely walk, followed by dinner at a posh restaurant and some dancing at a club. She had been looking forward to it all week but she would need to rein herself in. She didn't want to appear too eager. That was a big no-no on a first date. She had dressed casually, a fluffy cotton skirt, plain pink t-shirt and ballet flats. She wore her hair down deliberately because she knew Ethan loved it that way.

As soon as she heard the knock, she raced to the door.

He stood there with a wide mischievous smile, holding a pretty bouquet of spring flowers. He looked damn good, sporting a distressed leather jacket and a plain white T. She couldn't help but smile as she took the flowers from him. "Why, thank you," she said. "This is so sweet."

"Is your mother home?" he asked with a smirk.

She looked at him wide-eyed. "Why? We're not..." Did he just want to get her into bed straight away?

He laughed, his hands in the pockets of his dark jeans. "No, I was just checking," he explained. "It's best if she could make herself scarce when your date picks you up. A girl who still lives with her Mom is not very sexy."

She stood there, open-mouthed.

What a jerk.

"Well, it is what it is," she scoffed. "I live with my Mom and I happen to love my Mom."

"Okay," he conceded. "Don't get your panties in a bunch," he teased. "Next, why don't we go to your room, so you can show me the teddy bears on your bed."

What an asshole.

"Oh, don't you wish," she snickered. "In your dreams."

He laughed a soft chuckle. "Oh no... in your dreams, I think."

What an arrogant bastard.

This was not starting out well at all. She stood straighter and lifted her chin to him. "Why don't you go out the door, and come back in so we can start over."

"I'm sorry," he said, soft baby-blues pleading forgiveness. "Don't take me so seriously. Let's start over."

She liked him when he groveled. "Sure. I'll give you a chance. But that was strike one, buddy."

He grinned. "Oh... feisty. I like it. That's exactly how you want to be on a first date. Show him who's boss."

She bit her bottom lip. "Me," she said. "That's who's boss."

As he walked her to the parking garage where his black vintage Jag was waiting for them, Ethan wondered how she managed to look so sexy wearing only a cotton skirt and t-shirt. It was that gorgeous hair of hers, cruelly teasing him. She smiled at him as he opened the passenger door for her. He shot her a tight grin, vowing to compose himself. He would not be sleeping with her tonight. He had already taken care of business in the shower just before their date and he was 'master of his domain', as the saying goes. He would have full control tonight.

He had decided to bring her to Kubota Gardens on the suggestion of his sister. He wanted to take her somewhere special. Meghan had told him it was a beautiful spot, and he had never been there before.

When they closed in on the big brass gates, he couldn't help but take in Kirsten's face. It was full of wonder. She was like a kid at a candy store. Most of the women he dated would be unimpressed. All they cared about were fancy restaurants, designer dresses and jewelry... and looking good. And they certainly did look amazing. But Kirsten was completely different. And he loved that about her.

Her wide smile was contagious and he had the crazy urge to suddenly kiss her right there at the entrance of Kubota Gardens. But of course, he didn't.

As they walked along the paved path, taking in the gorgeous greenery, he realized this was the perfect opportunity to get to know her better. "Have you always lived in Seattle?"

"Yep. Born and raised. You?"

"Me too."

"You grew up with your mother?"

"Yes... my mother had me in her mid-twenties. She hooked up shortly with a drummer. She met him when she went to see his band play one night with her friends. He was gorgeous as she tells me," she went on. "But when she got pregnant with me, he didn't stick around. What a bastard, right?"

Ethan listened attentively, wanting to interrupt, but he was rather interested.

"She and I became best friends over the years," she went on, tilting her head as she walked next to him. Every now and then, he would glance her way. She took in the beauty surrounding them, but he couldn't have cared less. She was the only beautiful thing to look at as far as he was concerned.

"My mother had quite a hard time raising me as a single mother..." she carried on, oblivious.

He had to stop her. He just had to. He didn't want to, but he had to. "I'm sorry, Kirsten, but I need to stop you right there."

She stopped cold and shot him a puzzled look.

"This is a first date. I don't need to hear your whole life story. I asked you one question. You talk too much." He regretted the words as soon as he saw her face fall. Why did he have to be such a jerk all the time? "What..." he tried to recover, "What I mean is you can't talk too much on a first date. It needs to be back and forth. You need to hold back and ask questions too."

She brought her hand to her mouth, mortified. "You're right. I was completely boring you. I'm being so self-absorbed."

He smiled at her and took her hand. "No... you're not. I was interested. But it's just advice, good to consider on a first date."

"You're right," she conceded. "You really are the master."

He laughed. "That's me... the master," he agreed with a soft chuckle, but he was definitely not feeling it. He was not a master. He was not in control. All he wanted to do was grab her, hide her away under a tree and kiss her senseless.

He was right. She was talking too much. Questions. She would ask him questions. "This place is huge. How did you hear about this place?"

"My sister," he told her. "It was designed by this Japanese horticulturist. It mixes Eastern and Western greenery. "

"Well, it's beautiful," she said, taking in the lush gardens, stream and waterfall. "It's very peaceful... tranquil."

"It would make me want to meditate... if I meditated."

She laughed. "I can't meditate either... I'm too wired all the time."

"You're like me."

"We're more alike than you think," she pointed out and shot him a sly smile. Damn, he was gorgeous today, in his casual wear.

He surprised her when he grabbed her hand. "That's the moon bridge over there," he told her as his eyes fixed the red half-moon shaped bridge in the distance.

"It's pretty," she said as she stepped closer to him. Suddenly, she craved the closeness, the scent of him. He gazed at her for a fraction of a second, and she could tell he felt the same.

When they got to the bridge, they stood at the top taking in the beautiful scenery. He inched closer and wrapped his arms gently around her waist. She closed her eyes as her body warmed. This was different than how he had touched her before. This was chaste, not wild and hot. It was sweet. She longed to see his face, his expression. She turned slowly towards him and he fixed her with a soft gaze.

He was going to kiss her. She could see it in his eyes. And how she wanted that kiss... When he leaned in and pressed his mouth against hers, her knees almost gave out. His kiss was soft... his lips sweet. When his tongue softly coaxed hers, she felt her whole body being consumed by that kiss. She wanted to get lost in him. But unfortunately, they were standing in a very public park with many people milling about – it was a beautiful busy day.

She didn't want to, but she had to pull away.

He smiled and she could have sworn he blushed a little. "Sorry," he offered. "I got caught in the moment," he told her. "A little early on in the date for a kiss, right?"

She smiled wide. "Right."

As they continued to walk, taking in the beautiful hills and valleys, the sky grew dark above them. When she followed him closely through the narrow stone paths, wrapped in lush foliage, she inched closer to him to feel safer. He turned to smile at her. And all she could think about was that kiss, and how she wanted it again. Suddenly, there was just the two of them in this secluded path, and she desperately wanted to pull him to her.

6

——————

I CAN'T LIE... IT WAS PRETTY FUN

He jerked around suddenly. "Did you feel that?"

Her eyes grew wide. "Feel what?" she asked, wondering if there were some weird spiders she should be afraid of.

"A drop of rain," he told her, gazing up at the sky. "A second ago... it was sunny."

She laughed. "This is Seattle."

He smiled wide. "Right." And then right on cue, it started pouring. They were somewhat protected by the heavy foliage but they would eventually have to make their way out of the park. Kirsten studied herself; cotton t-shirt and light skirt. She was definitely not dressed for rain.

A huge grin stretched across his cheeks as he took her hand. "Let's make a run for it."

She bit her lip and nodded. They scurried their way off the path, and when they reached the big wide open space, they raced along the paved path. He led her but was careful not to run too fast, as if he could tell exactly how fast her small legs could carry her. She felt high on life, like a little kid. When was the last time she had run like this?

Suddenly, he veered off the path and she wondered where he was taking her. But then she quickly spotted the weeping blue cedars and she knew he was leading her to their protective shelter. Once they were refuged from the rain, he pulled her close to him. His eyes sparkled under his wet locks. His smile was more beautiful than she had ever seen it when he laughed. "You're drenched."

She swept her hand against her soaked locks. She stared down at her shirt which had now become completely see-through, the lace of her pretty bra evident. When she looked up, he was staring at her.

But the playful spark had faded from his eyes, replaced by a crazy intensity. She eyed him from top to bottom, taking in his toned shoulders and abs under the wet fabric of his shirt. God, he was gorgeous. Suddenly she wanted him right there, under the weeping cedar. How crazy. He pulled her in and took possession of her mouth with his, biting her bottom lip slightly. She let her body surrender completely. This was a different kind of kiss. This wasn't sweet at all. And she loved it. She buried her hands in his wet hair, wanting more. He grabbed her leg and pulled her even closer, grinding against her. It felt so good. They were losing control.

She tore herself from him again. She hated having to pull away. This was getting intense. The chemistry between them was through the roof. She couldn't remember ever having this kind of spark with Logan, or anyone else for that matter. But she needed to contain herself, and act like a lady. "I'm sorry," she breathed as she took a step back and stood at a safe distance.

He smiled. She was glad to see he wasn't upset. "You're right. I'm sorry," he told her. "I keep doing that." He smirked. "And that's not even part of the lesson."

She smiled. "I can't lie... it was pretty fun," she admitted, still a little breathless. "I'd like to do that again."

He grabbed her hand. "Me too. We're not too far. Let's race to the car."

They sprinted like children to the car and when they finally made it, they were drenched, rain dripping onto the leather seats of his vintage Jag. They smiled wide at each other and she wanted him again, but when he started the engine, eyes on the road, she knew he was being a good boy... for once. She sighed at the thought. She much preferred it when he misbehaved.

When she got home, she raced to her room and got out of her wet cold clothes. She checked her watch and realized there would be no time to dry her hair. She simply pinned it up and stuck a jeweled flower barrette in it. She chose a pretty red dress to complete the outfit. It was very 'Pretty Woman'. She couldn't count the many times her mother had made her watch that movie as a teenager. She had enjoyed the whole Cinderella theme of the movie but hadn't failed to notice the very messed-up message it sent. She'd always been extremely realistic and matter-of-fact about relationships and love... until now.

Why was Ethan making her feel this weak? She was usually so in control, but with him, she felt so unhinged. She felt like he could destroy her with a single false move, and that scared the hell out of her. As she stared at her reflection, she reminded herself. "Ethan Fox is a player," she whispered. "He might be the most amazing kisser on the planet, but he's definitely not the guy you fall in love with. Don't forget that, Kirsten." She felt a little silly talking to herself like this, but she needed to say the words out loud. She needed to get a hold of herself.

As soon as she stepped out of her mother's loft, she saw him standing at her door, looking amazing in a fitted dark suit, two button jacket with only one button done up. Did he know what he was doing to her?

Damn.

"You look amazing," he offered with a smirk. "The teacher approves."

She smiled. "Does he, now?" she asked playfully. "You look amazing too."

He inched closer and her breath hitched. Was he going to kiss her again? He pressed a finger seductively against her thigh and pulled the fabric up slowly. The long hem of her dress lifted off the ground to reveal her red strappy heels, a pair she had borrowed from her mother.

"I like the shoes too," he told her, gazing down at her feet. "But they could be one or two inches higher."

She scowled. "Do you have any idea how uncomfortable four or five inch heels are?"

He laughed. "And the hair should be down, but I understand, under the circumstances, why it's up."

She glared at him. "You don't like my up-do?"

"No, I love it. You look very beautiful," he tried to explain. "Hair worn down is sexier, that's all. Men imagine their hands lost in it while they're fucking you."

She stiffened at his words. They had taken her by surprise. She was feeling a little daring when she asked him, "How about you Mr. Fox? Did you have those thoughts when I wore my hair down around you?"

His grin was mischievous when he said, "Every single time."

THE RESTAURANT WAS beautiful with its floor-to-ceiling windows offering paranomatic views of the sun setting over Seattle. Kirsten told herself she needed to bring her mother here. Why had she never set foot in this place before?

The sophisticated hostess led them to their table, a pristine spot right by the fireplace. As she sat down, Kirsten took in the impressive stone structure and its warm flames. She couldn't help but appreciate the warmth and coziness of the place.

As Ethan sat across her and shot her a dazzling smile, she felt a little like Cinderella with her Prince. But how she had always hated the Cinderella story. It essentially told little impressionable girls across the world that all their dreams could be fulfilled by one man. Please. And again, she reminded herself how all of this, the beautiful restaurant, the gorgeous man, the dress and the candlelight... was all fantasy. And she was the girl with her feet firmly planted on the ground.

Ethan couldn't stop looking at her. She was so precious. Precious was not a word he ever used to describe the many women who have been part of his life. Sexy, hot as hell, gorgeous, wild, fun... But precious was new for him. He didn't quite know why, but he had the urge to keep her close by his side, to protect her and love her. Of course, he still wanted her naked, panting and begging while he fucked her into oblivion, but he also wanted to cherish her. He wondered what in the hell and the heavens was wrong with him as he perused the menu.

He had been here many times before. It was his go-to to impress a woman. And he was glad when it seemed to work for Kirsten as well. He hadn't failed to notice the spark in her eye when she took in the space. He wasn't sure why but he really cared what she thought. And for the first time in a long time, sitting in this fabulous restaurant, he was a little nervous.

He was impressed by the way she conducted herself. She was all class, and relatively relaxed, shooting him a seductive smile here and there. There wasn't much to teach. The only lesson here was to show her that dinner is all part of the foreplay. It's about playful banter, seductive looks, and fun.

He was usually so good at this but tonight he was at a complete loss for words. As she enjoyed her scallops, he dug into his rack of lamb, and wondered when he had become such a pussy. Where was his damn mojo?

"So Ethan," she started between bites of her salad. "Have you been here often?"

"Uh..." he faltered. Of course he had. "Yep, a few times."

She smiled wide. "A lot, I presume. I bet this is where you take all the ladies to impress them. It's quite romantic."

She was so on to him. He simply shot her a tight smile and chose to remain speechless.

"It's a slam-dunk I bet," she went on in a teasing tone. "Once you wine and dine them in this place, I'm sure they're a sure thing."

Now, she was starting to irritate him a bit. He suddenly had the urge to spar a little, to work her up. He smirked, nice and long. "Yep, it is. I usually have their legs wrapped around me by ten o'clock."

She cocked a brow. "Nice and easy. I'm sure they all fall for the whole Cinderella special. Candlelight dinner, a little dancing... And then a fuck-fest."

He was taken aback by her choice of words. He had never heard her utter the word with such venom. She was angry and hostile, and he kind of liked that.

"Yep, that's pretty much how it goes," he said, intent on working her up even more. He enjoyed seeing that fire in her eyes.

"Well, I'm not that stupid," she told him, all business. "There will be no fuck-fest tonight. I know your game and I'm not falling for it."

He smiled, putting down his fork. He had all but abandoned his meal. "Jeez, Kirsten, let me tell you something for your own good. You are doing terribly at this date."

She laughed out loud. "How so?"

"You're so defensive. You need to loosen up. So yeah, I want to fuck you. Just enjoy it for fuck's sake," he carried on in a whisper, a little worked up. She was driving him crazy. "If I recall correctly, you seemed to enjoy every second when we fucked on my sofa. And I'm pretty sure you'd love to do it again."

She sucked in a deep breath, at a loss for words. And he knew he had her. She couldn't argue his logic. He was right.

"What I'm saying is that on a date, don't think too much. That's probably the number one rule. Just have fun with it. Be in the moment."

She looked up from her plate. "Sorry, I keep forgetting this is supposed to be a lesson. Please go on and lavish me with all your wisdom, Sir."

He was both amused and annoyed by her snarkiness. But she looked so cute when she teased him like this, he had to let it slide.

All hard feelings where forgiven when they shared a luscious chocolate sauce covered brownie and she licked the chocolate off of his spoon. He couldn't get at her to touch her, but how he wanted to. She looked as delicious as the dessert.

Where had the sweet Ethan she was with at Kubota Gardens gone? In his place, was the usual arrogant ass she'd known for a long time. The womanizer, Seattle's most eligible bachelor. She didn't like him much but she had to admit, she loved the idea of him having his way with her. Despite herself, she was insanely attracted and drawn to the enigmatic Ethan Fox. What was wrong with her? She was smarter than that.

The nightclub was magical and sexy. And suddenly, a martini in hand, Kirsten felt loose. When was the last time she had gone out clubbing, dancing? She honestly couldn't remember. She decided to take Ethan's advice and just let go, enjoy the moment and have fun. She and Ethan were both way overdressed for the place but that made it even more fun. She felt like a socialite who had crashed a hip happening party.

She stood close to the bar while Ethan ordered them drinks. She reveled in the luscious space with its luxurious velvet red curtains and crystal chandelier. She couldn't believe how crowded the place was, sweaty bodies coming together like a tin of sardines. Every night, this kind of thing was happening, while she sat at home with a book. She suddenly wished she had gone out more. But all she needed at the time were her books and Logan. And look where she was now, she mused, a bystander, looking in from the outside, studying everything she had missed.

She hadn't noticed him staring at her, which was surprising because he was hard to miss. Tall, dark and handsome and... bearded. He was dressed up like her, standing all by his lonesome. And he fixed her like he meant business. She jerked her gaze away as soon as she realized he was looking at her. She really didn't know how to handle such situations.

She searched for Ethan and spotted him still at the bar. She ventured another look at the tall, dark stranger and he shot her a glorious smile. The man was gorgeous. More than gorgeous. He had that 'je-ne-sais-quoi', like he didn't quite belong there, as if he belonged somewhere better. She smiled shyly as he closed in on her.

"How are you?" he asked, the words laced with what she guessed was a European accent. She had been right. He didn't quite belong there.

She smiled politely. "I'm great. Thank you," she replied, tilting her head up. He was so tall, even taller than Ethan. She wasn't sure if she could handle taller than Ethan, but then she spotted the wide grin stretched across the man's beautiful face, and decided that she could. She definitely could climb that tree. "How are you?"

"Good," he said and inched his way even closer. "Better now."

"Where are you from?" She was dying to know.

"I am from Argentina," he told her. "I am here for work."

Ooohhh... not European. South American. Even better.

He extended his large hand to her. "My name is Antonio."

She smiled wide as she started to feel more comfortable. He wasn't sleazy... but rather sweet. "I'm Kirsten," she offered with a firm handshake. So far the night was going well.

She hadn't even noticed Ethan walk up to her, when he handed her an appletini. He caught her by surprise and she fumbled a little. "Oh... hi Ethan, this is Antonio," she offered, flustered. "This is my friend, Ethan," she explained to Antonio and noticed his face fall at the sight of the beautiful Ethan Fox. The man knew he had his competition cut out for him, and he didn't seem like the type who appreciated the challenge. She wanted to tell him she was single and available and not to worry at all about the gorgeous arrogant man with his arm now wrapped possessively around her waist.

Ethan took in the tall foreign man looming over him, and he pulled Kirsten closer and leaned in to press his mouth against the shell of her ear. "You're not going home with him," he whispered.

Kirsten sucked in a long breath. How dare him. Who did he think he was? She didn't belong to him. She was a free woman, for the first time in a long time. And damn if she wasn't going to enjoy it.

"I'll go home with whomever I damn wish," she scoffed, just loud enough for him to hear.

"Kirsten..." he said condescendingly. "You can't just go home with any guy you meet. I'm looking out for you. I'm keeping you safe."

"Bullshit." She was getting really peeved now. "You just want me all to yourself."

He laughed, and took a sip of his foreign beer.

The beautiful Antonio shot her another sweet smile and gently made his exit.

"You didn't even let me talk to him. You just barged in and marked your property. The guy probably thinks we're getting married tomorrow."

His annoying dimples made their appearance as he grinned widely. "Aren't we? I'm game if you are."

She rolled her eyes. "Be serious for a minute. I thought this was all supposed to be part of the lesson," she went on. "I wasn't planning to go home with the man, but it would have been nice just to talk to him. But you didn't even give me the chance to do that. How am I supposed to learn how to talk to a man, if you won't let me?" She knew she made an excellent point and he would have a hard time arguing her logic.

He bit his lip. "I'm sorry. I just didn't like the looks of him. He seemed like a sleaze ball."

She smiled. "You mean he was a little too gorgeous, and tall and seductive. I'm starting to see how this works," she carried on. "You'd like me to cut my teeth into a nice wholesome boy with a friendly smile and golf shirt, someone who probably wouldn't be able to give me an orgasm."

His face broke into a smile. "God, it's like you're a mind-reader."

"I'm right, aren't I... you were jealous."

He shrugged and pulled her closer. He fixed her with those amazing eyes of his, like he knew how powerful they were. Panties-melting eyes. "Why would I be jealous? I'm obviously the type you like, the guy who can make you come... twice now," he whispered against her ear. "And I'd like to do it again."

His words aroused her and she was speechless as she stood close to him. Yes, she had liked the looks of Antonio, but he didn't have the effect on her that Ethan had. She was brought back to the first time she had met him at the loft building.

She was carrying a bunch of books for a writing project she'd been working on, a modern retelling of Jane's Austen's *Pride & Prejudice*, a fan fiction of sorts. She had dropped her books, and had been a fumbling mess when she spotted those eyes. And to make matters worse, some of the books afore-mentioned were erotica. So embarrassing. But he hadn't seemed to notice the books. His eyes were on her, and only her. It was love at first sight. And then he opened his mouth, and said something arrogant and pouf! Just like that, the feeling was gone.

But then the erotic dreams had started.

"You feel like dancing?" he asked, not so much a question. He dragged her to the dance floor, his smile contagious. Kirsten recognized the song. It was one she sang along to every time she heard it on the radio.

Damn, he was a good dancer too, she realized as he pulled her seductively to him. Her hips swayed against his. He trailed a hand to her head, and unpinned her hair clip. Her hair fell thick and luscious over her shoulders. He pinned the clip on the lapel of his jacket and shot her a smile as he trailed a hand through her locks. And suddenly, she felt so sexy, sexier than she ever had. She pulled him closer and started grinding against him to the beat of the music. She gazed up at him, her face close to his. He bit down a smile, and pressed himself even closer against her, as close as they could get.

She felt his erection against her belly and it aroused her beyond words. She closed her eyes, wanting to take this party elsewhere. They were dancing slowly now, and he pressed his lips against hers, fully consuming her mouth. As their tongues danced and twirled, their pace slowed down. The music and the lights receded. They had fallen into another realm. They were in their own world now. The taste of him, the feel of him. She couldn't get enough.

He pulled away from her. "I need to take you home," he breathed, the words buried in her hair.

Oh yes... please do.

When Ethan took the keys from the valet, she wondered how long the drive to their place was. She couldn't wait. He had worked her up so much on the dance floor, she had the urge to climb all over him right there in his vintage Jag. But this was valet parking after all. That naughty business would just have to wait, she mused, biting her lip. She hated waiting. Delayed gratification was not her thing at all. He shot her a wicked smile as they drove off into the beautiful nightscape of Seattle. And she felt so alive.

She held her heels by the strap, walking barefoot. "Heels are such a pain," she told him as they stepped off the elevator. "You're lucky you're a man and don't have to suffer the modern tortures of womanhood."

As they reached the end of the hall, he pulled her in front of his door. This is it, she thought. He looked at her with longing but his smile told another story – it was tight, all-business. "Would you like to come in for a drink?"

Hell, yeah, she thought. She knew that was code for 'sex'. "I would love to," she replied with her best seductive smile.

He shook his head. "No, you wouldn't," he said simply. "You don't want to accept an invitation like that on the first date," he explained, all business. "The second maybe, definitely the third... but not the first."

Her heart sank. He was brushing her off.

"It tells me you're easy. And no man worth his salt likes an easy woman," he went on, completely oblivious to her inner turmoil. This little speech was destroying her. "We men like the thrill of the chase... the mystery," he plowed on. "We like a woman who plays a little hard to get," he explained. "You want a man who desires you, who fantasizes about having you, who becomes a little obsessed with you," he carried on, his expression dead-serious. "You don't want to give all the goods away too early. The man will lose interest real fast and move on."

Oh my God. Was that what he was trying to tell her? That he had already lost interest since she had so easily let him have her over the back of his sectional sofa? Been there. Done that. Time to move on.

She could literally feel her heart being crushed, the heaviness fully consuming her. She was on the verge of tears, careful to measure her words and keep her tone even, master her response to the heart-wrenching rejection because above all else, she didn't want him to know she cared. "I see," she said. The less words, the better. "Good lesson," she added with a nod, staring at the floor. "I suppose I'll see you around. Thanks," she added quickly as she scurried away to her door like a little mouse.

"I had fun," he called out. "I hope you did too."

She nodded quickly and retreated into the haven of her mother's loft. And as soon as she shut the door, she collapsed to her knees and let her tears fall quietly, careful not to wake her mother.

She should have known. She knew all along what an arrogant asshole he was, a narcissist who gets off on women admiring him, wanting him, always in search of someone new to stroke his ego. She cursed herself for falling, even when she had all the facts at her disposal. She had known who he was. And yet... she couldn't help herself. He had a pull on her, he excited her, made her want to become someone she wasn't.

She told herself she should have never gotten involved in the first place. Now, she regretted that moment, the moment she let him in. She had shown him all her vulnerabilities, and all he had done was shoot her down, without a moment's hesitation. And God... she couldn't get away from him. The man lived next door. There would be no clean break here like there had been with Logan.

What a horrible nightmare.

7

———

SEE? YOU WIN EITHER WAY

Ethan kicked off his shoes and slouched on his sofa. He rubbed his face raw, trying to shake the image of her out of his mind. He had done it. He had promised himself he wouldn't sleep with her again, and he hadn't. It was time to end this little game. At first he thought it would be fun. But he could clearly see that she was developing feelings for him, getting attached.

And he certainly wasn't helping the situation, kissing her left and right. It was one thing when they were just fucking on the back of his sofa. He had done that kind of thing so many times with women, but never with a woman like Kirsten. And he had kissed his share of women too. After all, kissing was usually the gateway to sex.

But he had never felt the way he felt when he kissed Kirsten. With her, it wasn't a means to an end. It was something he wanted to do forever. He shook his head, trying to clear the vision of them on the moon bridge, under the weeping cedars and on the dance floor at the club. How he had wanted to take her home, but he couldn't go there.

Sure, they had had sex already, but it had been just that. Sex.

And he knew he no longer wanted just sex with Kirsten. If he had let her into his loft, he would have wanted to get her completely naked, and lay her on his bed, kiss and taste her everywhere, reveling in every inch of her body. And that sounded an awful lot like making love, and they couldn't go there, because if they did, they would both probably never recover.

He had to make an action plan. He would end the lessons and tell her he thought she was doing great and would do more than fine when she was ready to enter the world of dating again. The thought of her dating other men drove him kind of crazy, but he was sure he would get over it shortly. As soon as he put some distance between the two of them, it would be easier to do so. He would try to avoid her at all costs, but he knew he would probably run into her once in a while at the elevators or walking to his door. That was unavoidable. Of course, he would make small talk, but he would be careful to keep it curt and not overly friendly.

It would all work itself out, his logical side told him, but his heart seemed to have second thoughts. He had never ever felt so empty. The last time he had been so upset was when his mother had left his family to run off with that idiot of an artist.

KIRSTEN WOKE UP AND UNFORTUNATELY, her thoughts traveled straight to the previous night's events. How she hated him. He was dead to her as far as she knew. The lessons were over. The friendship was over. Of course, she would probably have to see the arrogant prick on a weekly basis, but vowed to ignore him. And if they happened to be standing by the elevators together, as they occasionally did, she would watch him step in, and she would wait for the next one. He was dead to her. Dead.

She dragged herself to the kitchen to make herself peanut butter and jelly toast, although she had no appetite. Lorraine was sitting at the kitchen table, working on another crossword puzzle. She shot her head up at the sight of her daughter. "How did it go last night?" she asked, eager. "Your date with Ethan?"

"Ugh," Kirsten grunted loudly. "It went awful. I hate him. And that's all I'm going to say about it."

Lorraine sat up straight. "What happened?" Apparently she hadn't quite heard her daughter when she said she didn't want to talk about it. Mothers do have selective hearing. Kirsten shrugged, not having the strength to deal with her mother. She knew Lorraine would never let it go. And part of her really wanted to share the way she was feeling, let it all out. She helped herself to coffee, abandoning her toast, and sat across Lorraine. "Well," she started, shoulders hunched. "We went for a wonderful walk at Kubota Gardens and we kissed and it was all very romantic... like a scene from one of your books.

Lorraine cocked a brow. "Sounds good so far."

"Then we got caught in the rain, and came home to change. We had dinner at this amazing restaurant, and we had a little fight but it was nothing."

Lorraine abandoned her crossword, her attention now fully devoted to her daughter.

"Then we went to a cool club and some gorgeous Argentinian hit on me. But Ethan put the kibosh on that pretty fast. He was so possessive."

"It's because he likes you," Lorraine chimed in. "It's obvious."

"I'm not so sure about that, Mom. Because when we got home, he didn't invite me in. He basically told me he had already had his glass of milk, and he had no more use for the cow."

Lorraine's mouth dropped open. "He did not," she exclaimed. "I don't believe it."

"That's basically what he said. He said I was too easy."

"You... easy?" she broke in. "That's ridiculous. What an arrogant asshole."

"Exactly," Kirsten agreed. Now they were on the same page.

"I'm so sorry I set the two of you up together. I really thought he was a good kid."

She smiled at her mother. "It's not your fault, Mom. He's very charming and he can fool the best of them."

Lorraine blew out a breath. "And here I was planning a double-date. With you and Ethan, and Max and I."

Kirsten smirked. "So, you're still seeing that boy-toy. Good for you, Mom."

"I know you don't quite approve, Kirsten."

"I do," she argued. "I do now. One of us might as well be having fun," she pointed out. "But I would forget all about the double-date."

"That's too bad. I thought it'd be fun," her mother told her. "We're going to a gastro-brewery nearby. It was Max's idea."

Kirsten smiled. "Yep, I got that." Somehow, she couldn't really picture her mother at a brewery-type eatery. Her mom was all about posh five-star restaurants with sleek white leather chairs and crystal chandeliers. "You have fun."

Lorraine pressed her manicured nail against her mouth. "But... perhaps, I could... Max has a friend who's single, and pardon my words... he's sex on legs."

Kirsten laughed out loud. "Sex on legs?" She almost choked on her coffee. "Really, Mom?"

"I'm telling you, Kirsten. I've only met him once. He's a sculptor and... absolutely delicious."

Kirsten could only stare at her mother, speechless.

"You see, Kirsten," Lorraine started, squaring her shoulders, and Kirsten knew Lorraine was gearing up for another one of her little eccentric talks. She smiled at the thought. She was always so entertained by these little tidbits of wisdom her mother so kindly offered.

"There are three types of men," Lorraine went on. "There's the one you want to take to your parents. And then, there's the one you want to drag to a dark corner and do sinful things with.

And of course, there are the ones who fall somewhere in the middle."

Kirsten stared at her mother, mouth agape. She was familiar with Lorraine's language and candor, but somehow she could never seem to get used to it.

Lorraine went on with a playful smile. "Now, Logan fell in the former category, and Ethan... Well, he was kind of in the middle. But this guy, Kirsten... I'm telling you... is definitely in the latter category. A 'dark corner' kind of guy."

"Well, hell, Mother," Kirsten finally managed to say. "Now you've got me absolutely dying of curiosity."

"We could all go together," Lorraine suggested, "and have a hell of a time."

Kirsten smiled. "No... absolutely not." She had had just about enough for a while.

"It could take your mind off things," Lorraine quickly countered with a mischievous smile.

The woman did have a point. Thinking about Ethan was driving her insane, and she just knew she wouldn't be able to get him off her mind for a long, long while. Especially when the jerk lived right next door. A distraction might just be what the doctor ordered. And if this guy was as gorgeous as her mother described, perhaps he could really get her mind off Ethan. He would probably end up being another jerk, but she was willing to do anything to make the pain she was feeling go away.

"Maybe..." she hesitated to say, wondering what she was getting herself into. Her mother's ideas weren't always the best.

"Fantastic," Lorraine cheered. "I'll make it happen. We'll have so much fun. Ethan who, right?"

Kirsten stood by the elevators, chewing on a nail. It had been a long day at work and she couldn't wait to get home, make some homemade pizza, and binge watch *Gilmore Girls* with her mother. She was almost in a good mood until...

He came walking in, larger than life, as he usually did. But this time, his usual smirk was absent. In its place, stretched a very tight smile. "Hi, dragonfly."

She couldn't believe he still called her that. It was for the best because every time the man uttered her name, she went a little weak at the knees. She sneered in his direction and didn't say a peep. He was not worth a single syllable.

"Listen, Kirsten," he said, all business, as they stepped into the elevator. She would have waited for the next one but she couldn't wait to get home, and her feet were killing her.

He pressed the button. "I've been thinking... it's probably best if we call off the lessons," he started, not quite making eye contact. "I think you're amazing and you'll be great whenever you decide to go on a date."

"Sounds good to me," she said without emotion.

"You find yourself a good decent man and you'll forget all about Logan."

These words were the straw that broke the camel's back. She couldn't stand his condescending overly polite tone. He was completely dismissing what they had shared with his fabricated civility. He was also implying that they were done and she would be best to find herself a man more in her league. What an arrogant prick. All of a sudden, she wanted to piss him off, make him jealous, and show him she wasn't the good girl he thought she was.

She laughed loudly as they exited the elevator. "That's not likely to happen," she told him with a flirty flip of her head. "Cole is many things, but good and decent is not one of them."

He jerked his head towards her, wide-eyed. "Who's Cole?"

"Oh," she said, pulling the clip out of her hair and letting her luscious mane fall over her shoulders. "He's a guy I'm dating."

Okay, so technically, she hadn't even met him yet, but they were going on a date in three days.

Kirsten smiled inwardly at Ethan's sudden concern.

"I didn't know you were dating anyone," he said. "How long have you been seeing this guy?"

She averted her gaze towards her door, avoiding his question. "I've gotta go. I'm making dinner."

"So what's this Cole like?"

She smiled, realizing she had his full attention. She couldn't believe she was playing these games. She really wasn't the type. But he had a way of turning her into a shallow, raving lunatic. "Cole is amazing. He's a sculptor, extremely passionate, and gorgeous as sin."

His face fell. She waited for him to utter a sardonic response but he was speechless. She waved good-bye as she turned the handle. As soon as she closed the door, a huge smile stretched across her face. Suddenly, the day had taken a better turn.

A SCULPTOR, Ethan mused. Why in the hell did it have to be a sculptor? She might as well have punched him in the gut when she told him she was seeing a gorgeous, passionate brooding artist. He hated the type. It was exactly the type who had stolen his mother from his father when Ethan was ten years old. And this had affected him deeply, every career move, every relationship, every friendship. He no longer trusted people. If his own mother could betray him, how could he trust anyone?

And he hadn't. Not until he had met Kirsten. She was different. She seemed sweet, genuine, the type who would never lie or play games, who simply didn't have the ability. But had he been wrong? Because all of a sudden, it seemed she was doing just that, playing games and taunting him.

It had been three hours since he'd spoken to Kirsten and he

just couldn't shake the vision of her with this other man, this 'Cole'. He imagined him tall, dark and handsome, with long hair down to his tattoo covered shoulders. He couldn't take it. He had to see this man for himself. He didn't know why he cared so much, why she was turning him into a pathetic crazy stalker. He had told himself he would stay away from her, but now all he could think about was her and this new man. It was driving him absolutely crazy. All he knew was that he was now on a mission.

It hadn't exactly required exemplary investigative skills to find out where they would be. It had simply been a matter of chatting up Lorraine in the elevator. The woman loved to talk. She told him they were all going to Brass Tacks on Friday night to have dinner. It would be easy enough to go check out this guy. Ethan had been there many times with colleagues and friends. He knew the place like the back of his hand. He would drag along a colleague for a late dinner, and 'accidentally' run into them.

KIRSTEN COULDN'T BELIEVE how nervous she was. But she told herself that she had reason to be. She had never been on a blind date before, and especially not one with a sinfully gorgeous man. She searched through her closet for something 'sexy but not too desperate'. She finally settled on a slick little blue dress, a cheap impulse purchase at Forever 21.

She decided to wear her hair down and as she brushed her locks, she realized this would be the perfect opportunity to practice the skills she had learned during her lessons with Ethan. The man had not been a complete waste. He had given her quite a few tips. She decided to take the jerk's advice and just have fun with it, and not think too much.

OH GOD...

For once, her mother hadn't been making up stories. The man was beautiful. He looked like Robert Pattinson's better looking brother. There was an intensity about him that left her breathless as he shook her hand. He wore a tattered t-shirt and worn jeans, a silver chain dangling from the pocket. Very 'homeless-chic'. Seriously, Kirsten thought, who needs designer clothing when you're this gorgeous. His hair was disheveled and his face scruffy, as if he had just literally gotten out of bed. As she shot him a smile, Kirsten wondered if in fact, he had just gotten out of bed. "It's nice to meet you, Cole."

His playful expression told her he liked what he saw. "Likewise," he offered. He had intelligent eyes and a deep voice. And despite the fact that he had only uttered a few words, she had the feeling he was smart, the type who knew all the great artists, and who could quote Ernest Hemingway.

Mmmmm.

"Well, let's go in, shall we?" Lorraine suggested as she held on to her very tall and handsome date's arm. Max seemed completely enamored with her, and Kirsten knew this was the real thing between them. She also knew it would probably not last very long, given the age difference and her mother's track record. But she was happy for her mother. Cole led her in with a hand pressed lightly at the small of her back.

The place was awesome. Industrial chic. All sleek woods and steel. A colorful bar, funky vintage bar stools and light fixtures added to the whole appeal. As soon as the perky hostess led them to their table, a worn slab of wood hanging over a wooden bench and two steel chairs, Kirsten knew the atmosphere here was casual. And she liked that. She didn't need the extra stress of sitting in a stuffy restaurant. A blind date was unnerving enough.

She and her mother took a seat on the comfy bench and as she sat down, Kirsten couldn't help but ogle Cole as he peeled off his distressed leather jacket. He had beautiful Celtic tattoos all over his arms. She had never been a fan of tattoos, but she liked his. She smiled at him, happy with the fact that she was quite familiar with Gaelic culture, having studied it in college. "Are you of Irish descent?" she asked. "Or Scottish?"

He smiled wide. "Both actually. Obvious, isn't it?"

"A little," she said. "Do you speak Gaelic?"

He laughed. "I like to think I do," he told her, "but I really don't."

She smiled. "I like to think I speak French," she replied, "but I really don't."

As they both laughed, she spotted her mother flashing her a wink. Damn, this was going well. She already liked this guy and she barely knew him.

Kirsten shook her head as she perused the menu. Such eccentric choices. She opted for a poutine. She was feeling quite indulgent. And she would even have a drink too, she decided. Tonight was a night to let loose and forget all about Ethan Fox.

But then, she almost had a coronary as she lifted her head from her menu. She was sure her mind was playing tricks on her. There, by the entrance, stood the enigmatic Ethan Fox, dressed in a sharp suit, flanked by two equally formally dressed men. They stood out like clowns at a funeral. What the hell was he doing here? When Lorraine spotted her expression, she turned her head toward the door. She jerked back. "I can't believe it."

Kirsten couldn't believe it either. She was speechless. In a city this large, offering so many restaurants, what were the odds of them being at the same place tonight? Slim to none, she deduced. The man was stalking her. As he took in the space, seemingly searching, and finally resting his gaze on her with a serious expression, it was confirmed. The man had followed her here. But how did he know?

"Mom," she said. "Did you tell him we'd be here tonight?"

Lorraine sat a little on edge. "Well..." she faltered. "I-I may have..."

"Mother," Kirsten scoffed. And all eyes at the table were on her. Even Cole seemed to know something was up. She drew a deep breath, determined to not let Ethan ruin her night. This place was plenty big enough. She would simply ignore him.

As Ethan followed the hostess to his table and flashed them a smile with a wave of his hand, Kirsten noticed a few ladies' heads turn. Of course, he would make heads turn, dressed like that. The man looked like an Hugo Boss ad. Kirsten scowled, determined to not let him affect her. Here she was, sitting with this super sexy, slightly-dangerous guy. Cole looked like the type who would be good under the sheets. She'd just have to focus on that.

As she nursed a gin and tonic, Kirsten tried to keep her focus on the man sitting across from her. They talked about their studies, Europe and Cole's current obsession, Italian artist Giovanni Boldini. This conversation was right up her alley, but damn, all she could think about was Ethan. She could see him in the back sitting with his two buddies and she wondered if he'd come up to say hello.

It seemed like their food order was taking forever to come. It was probably because Kirsten suddenly wanted to be anywhere but there. She smiled as Cole talked her ear off and she sat straighter when she saw Ethan approaching. She had been expecting him.

He flashed his charismatic smile. "Hello, ladies," he offered. "You two look in fine form tonight."

"Hello, Ethan," Lorraine replied, her tone uncharacteristically cold. Kirsten shot him a tight smile. It was awkward to say the least. Ethan paused, as if analyzing the situation and trying to understand why he wasn't receiving the usual cheerful reception. He offered his hand to Cole. "I'm Ethan. I'm the next door neighbor."

"Oh," Cole said, as if finally understanding. Kirsten thought she spotted a flicker of relief, like he had concluded in response to that simple statement that Ethan was no competition. "I'm

Cole. I'm a good friend of Max's," he explained with a tilt of his head.

Lorraine broke in. "Max is my good friend," she offered by way of explanation. 'Good friend' was what she called Max. She couldn't bring herself to say 'boyfriend', which in her defense, would have sounded a little juvenile and ridiculous. Ethan shook Max's hand. "Well, it's nice to meet you all. This is a great place, isn't it?"

Please just leave, Kirsten thought. She really didn't have the patience for this. Visions of their last encounter and how he so cruelly dismissed her danced around in her head. She crossed her arms and lifted her nose, wanting to tell him off but not finding the words.

"I come here all the time," he went on. "Usually after work, with colleagues."

"I bet you do," Kirsten added. *You psycho stalker.*

He flashed her a playful grin, seemingly completely oblivious to the fact that she now despised him. "Up for a game of foosball later," he asked. "There's a game at the back."

"I doubt it," she snickered.

"C'mon, it'll be fun," he told her. "Remember what I told you about having fun. You need to let loose once in a while."

She had the urge to let loose alright, let loose and punch him in the face.

"I'm coming to get you later," he added with a wink, and despite everything she had told herself, her heart skipped a beat. Traitor heart.

Kirsten could barely eat her poutine. She had completely lost her appetite. Anger, nerves, anticipation... She didn't know exactly why she suddenly felt slightly nauseous. How could one man affect her body so much? She hated the fact that he still managed to get to her. How long would it be until he was finally completely out of her system?

As she shared a delicious fudge cake with Cole, she couldn't help but appreciate how well the date was going. He was every-thing she could have wanted, sweet, kind, sexy and smart. He seemed like a bit of a drifter, a dreamer. But that was not neces-sarily a bad thing since she was quite the opposite. And as they say, opposites attract.

She was digging into the fudge cake when Ethan popped up right next to her and made her jump a little. This time, she hadn't seen him coming. "So about that game of foosball?"

She shook her head. "Sorry, kind of busy."

He tilted his head. "Well, I'm sure Cole here won't mind," he said. "You don't mind do you, Cole?"

"Not at all."

"See, he doesn't mind," Ethan said and the next second, he was grabbing her by the arm and practically dragging her to the back of the restaurant. She struggled to keep up with him in her chunky heels. How she hated him.

"We need to hurry before someone steals the game," he told her as they raced by tables.

"I was in the middle of dessert," she pointed out. "And also in the middle of a very wonderful conversation."

"Discussing the merits of tattoos, I'm sure," he replied. And she didn't miss his sardonic tone.

When they inched near the aforementioned game, she could literally feel the anger rushing to her cheeks. "What is your problem?"

He jerked his head again and ignored her question. "Just one game. If you win, I'll leave you alone."

She was intrigued by the proposition, but also concerned. "But what if you win?"

"Um... let's see," he said, pondering the industrial lofty ceiling. "I'll still leave you alone and let you get back to nose-ring."

She sneered at him.

His grin was playful, and mildly annoying. "See? You win either way."

As they started playing, she was determined to beat his ass. She had a fair amount of practice at the game, having played with Logan often. He had a game at his place. She did love it which was why Ethan had so easily been able to convince her to play. It had absolutely nothing to do with how amazing he looked in that suit.

"You're pretty good at this."

She smirked as she scored. Two against one for her. "I know."

"So this thing with Cole," he ventured. "How serious is it?"

She rolled her eyes. It wasn't any of his business. "Why do you care?"

He shrugged, letting another goal in. "I don't."

"Could have fooled me."

He kept playing, not looking at her.

"Why are you here?" she asked, point-blank. "This can't just be a coincidence."

"I told you," he tried to explain but she knew better. "I come here all the time with my buddies."

"Sure."

He slammed his hand against the side of the game when she scored again. She was crushing him. "Fuck," he cursed. "All right. I admit it... I wanted to see the guy you were dating."

"Why?" she asked. They had both stopped playing. "Why do you care who I date? You obviously have no interest in me. I practically threw myself at you and you just brushed me off, like some dirt off your shoe."

He fixed her with wide eyes. "I didn't..."

"And then you basically told me that you've had me and I was all used up."

"I said no such thing, Kirsten," he argued, eyes wide. "What in the world are you talking about?"

She was on the verge of tears when she went on, despite knowing that she should just walk away and go back to that delicious slice of man-pie waiting for her. "You didn't want me. You said I was too easy. And the next day, you called the whole thing off."

He made his way closer to her and took her hand. His eyes were full of sorrow when he said, "I'm sorry, Kirsten. That's not how I wanted you to feel. I just thought you and I... we were getting a little too close. And I don't want to hurt you—"

"But you did," she cried. Tears had officially made their way to the surface.

"I didn't want to give you the wrong idea, Kirsten," he tried to explain. "You know me... I don't do relationships. I'm in it for the fun. I like to play. And you..." he went on, his gaze fixing hers.

"And me... what about me?"

8

I KNOW YOU WOULD NEVER HURT ME

God, she was so beautiful, standing in that slutty little dress, her eyes wet with emotion, with the pain he had caused. He had done exactly what he was trying not to do. He had hurt her deeply. She had completely misunderstood him. He didn't think she was cheap, easy. In fact, it was quite the opposite. He thought she was precious, special, and too good for the likes of him. He wanted to take her in his arms and reassure her, kiss her pain away.

He knew he was only getting deeper, but he couldn't walk away. And he didn't want to. He took her by the hand and led her to the back. She eyed him curiously, and he knew she didn't quite trust him, but yet, she still followed him. They walked past the old vintage trunk coffee table and piano. They inched closer to the fireplace, the odd piece which looked like it belonged on the set of a sitcom show. She shot him a quizzical look as she studied the fireplace, knowing it wasn't real. He smiled at her playfully, pressed his palm against the fireplace, and shared a well-kept secret. Her eyes grew with fascination, like a kid's at an amusement park. "What the hell?"

As he turned the fireplace façade inward, toward the secret hidden room, he held her hand and brought her in with him.

As soon as they found themselves in complete seclusion in the small dark private room, he pulled her closer to him. He couldn't help himself. She was so beautiful, and he just wanted to revel in her. She stared at him with such a mix of emotions in her eyes, he didn't know what to think. What she mad? What she confused? In lust? In love? All he knew was that he definitely had a strong effect on her. He had a strong hold of her and didn't want to let go. But he felt her resistance and eased up on her.

"What in the hell are you doing?" she snapped. Okay, it was official. She was mad. Livid.

"I wanted to talk."

"I'm so sick of this hot and cold act," she hissed, completely worked up. "One minute you push me away, and the next you're all over me and squeezing me into dark little rooms."

He liked seeing her all worked up like this. She was so damn cute when she was angry.

"This might be the kind of thing that gets you off, but it's not for me. I don't like playing games, Ethan," she scoffed. "And if you think we're going to end up doing it on that sofa, you've got another thing coming."

She had noticed the sofa and her mind had gone there. She obviously was thinking about it as much as he was. He pulled her closer and trailed his finger along her thigh. He was suddenly losing his mind. He was dying to touch her, to feel her, discover her wetness, see how turned on she was by all this. Because he was sure she was.

"Stop it," she pleaded, a hand on his. "This is like living in a damn Taylor Swift song. I can't take the drama anymore."

He had never seen her so angry before and he could tell she meant business. He reluctantly let go.

She fixed him with the saddest eyes he'd ever seen. "You don't want me," she pointed out. "But you don't want anyone else to have me either. Please let me go, and let me move on with my life."

She was right. He had to let go. And he was absolutely speechless. He watched her push the fireplace around and disappear into the bright busy restaurant. He took in the dark cozy space around him and couldn't help but imagine all the delicious filthy things he could have been doing to her, had she stayed.

Kirsten made her way back to her table, a little unsteady on her feet. She was shaken. When he had pressed her against that façade and brought her into that secret room, her breath had hitched and an ache had traveled from her stomach, to down below. She had wanted him so much. She had wanted him to hike up her dress and rip her panties off. And she would have let him, if he had. But she had been strong. She didn't want him to hurt her anymore, didn't want to give him that power.

She sat across Cole and flashed him an artificial smile. She grinned at her mother, who seemed to know what was up.

"How did the game go?" Lorraine asked, polishing off her dessert.

"Good," Kirsten said. "I beat him."

She took in the smiles all around and vowed to forget all about Ethan Fox, his pretty words and that sexy little secret room.

But as much as she wanted to forget all about him, she was simply incapable of doing so. Ethan was all she could think about as she chatted with Cole. It didn't make sense. Here was this beautiful sexy man in front of her, and all she could think about was this other man, this frustrating, arrogant, mind-fucking jerk. She had absolutely no control over her thoughts. Her body craved him like a drug, and no alternative would do.

Later that night, she slipped off her dress, and it pooled to the floor as she studied her reflection in the wall mirror. She was wearing a pretty lace see-through bra and panties. Her hair fell softly over her breasts, and her skin was glowing. She felt the pressure build within her, that all-consuming desire to be touched, cherished... to be taken.

One last time.

Ethan tossed and turned. He had gone to bed early in the hopes of falling into slumber and forgetting all about her. Thoughts of her had been driving him wild all night. When she had left him in that secret room, he knew she had been right, that he shouldn't be running after her. He understood he had to let her go. He wasn't the man for her. She deserved someone better.

As he joined his buddies back at the table, he tried to enjoy himself, forget all about her. But all he could think about was her and that guy Cole. The man was everything he deplored, an indulgent, carefree artist, the type who probably owned an extensive collection of vinyl LPs and typed letters to his grandmother on a vintage typewriter. Yes, the tattoos were bad-ass, Ethan conceded, but the guy was a pussy as far as he was concerned.

He pictured Cole's hole-in-the-wall apartment, filthy, messy, old warped books stacked against the wall. And that only led to visions of Cole seducing Kirsten, playing a folk song for her on his beaten-up acoustic guitar. And damn it if the guy didn't have a good voice too. Of course Kirsten would be getting all hot and bothered. That's when the asshole would make his move, press her against the wall, hike up that slutty little dress she was wearing, and rip off her panties, basically doing everything to her that he had wanted to do to her. And then the jerk would kneel to the floor and go down on her, and her breathless moans would echo off the walls as he made her come.

These images were not helping. They were slightly arousing, but also frustrating as hell.

Damn you, nose-ring asshole.

ETHAN PRESSED a pillow against his face and smothered himself for a second or two. Temporary death would have been almost welcomed at this point, but there was no such thing as temporary death. How he would enjoy a nice coma, he mused, staring up at the dark ceiling, the lights from the city reflecting across it. He would from then on, be condemned to seeing someone he can't have, seeing her with men who would get to touch her, hold her... taste her. He realized he was never getting any sleep. It was a good thing the next day was a Saturday and he would be able to sleep in a little. He figured he'd probably still go to work after a late breakfast to keep his mind off her, and maybe to the gym afterwards to work off his frustrations.

When he heard the knock at his door, he thought it was his imagination. Who could be calling at this hour? But when he heard it again, he bounced off the bed. He made his way cautiously to the front door, wearing only his Calvin boxers. God, the last thing he needed right now was a problem with his apartment, or a loved one. His thoughts jumped instantly to Meghan. He honestly didn't know if he could handle something happening to his sister.

He may have been tall and built, but he was still looking into that peep hole. His heart skipped a beat when he saw her face. He opened the door in a hurry, wanting to know why she was there, at this hour. As soon as he saw her expression, he knew why she was there. He got hard in record time, wanting to fully devour her. He took her in from head to toe. She was wearing a sweet plush house coat, falling just below the knee, covered with ladybugs. It wasn't particularly sexy, but he knew underneath she was probably naked.

He pulled her in and slammed the door shut behind them. He pressed her hard against himself and took her mouth with a vengeance, unwillingly biting her bottom lip in the process. But she didn't seem to mind. She hung off him, and clawed at his back as his fingers got tangled in her hair. She smelled so amazing and her hair was so soft. This was already heaven, and he was nowhere near inside her. He wanted to savor her, to make this last. He didn't want to think about all the reasons he shouldn't be doing this. He just wanted to enjoy her.

He grasped the tie of her robe and she pulled away. "Just one night," she whispered, breathless. "One last time." Her beautiful eyes were so dark, almost haunting. There was a flicker of emotions he couldn't miss; fear, doubt, confusion, but mostly desire. She ached for him, and he loved that. He wanted her so much too. "Not here," she told him. "In your bed."

"In my bed," he said, his words heavy with desire. The thought of pressing her against the soft mattress of his bed, reveling in her body, slowly enjoying every inch of her, drove him crazy. He pressed his mouth against the base of her neck, tasting her, working the tie of her robe. They would get to his bed in a minute, but right now he wanted her naked. He had never seen her nude but couldn't count the times he had fantasized about it.

He pulled the robe open and swallowed hard when he saw the sexy two-piece she was wearing, a see-through fabric trimmed with dark lace and accentuated with little bows. She had managed to be both sweet and sexy. That was Kirsten in a nutshell. She bit down a playful smile and that only made him crazier. God, he wanted her. "Are you trying to kill me?"

"Of course not." She smiled. "Because if you were dead, then you couldn't please me, could you?"

Damn. He lifted and pressed her against the wall in a fraction of a second. Her robe had fallen off her shoulders and he bit her flesh gently. Her teeth scraped against his jaw as she frantically searched for his mouth. He'd never seen her like this. She was completely unhinged. She needed to be thoroughly fucked... and now. This was a most urgent matter.

He carried her to his room, her legs wrapped around his hips. She was light as a feather as they made their way to his bed. She bounced off the mattress when he threw her. He wasted no time in freeing her from the pink robe. And she surprised him when she peeled off his boxers and ran her hands over his ass. And when she held him in her hands, he thought he might just completely lose it. He had to shut his eyes and talk himself down. He pulled away softly. "I want to be with you..." he whispered. "Inside you."

"Me too," she said, breathless. Her soft pleading voice was not helping his composure. He had been with many women, but had never sensed such pure desire.

"But not quite yet," he told her. "I want to savor you, discover you."

She pressed a smile against his cheek. "I like the thought of that. I want to discover you too," she said, the words sweet like honey. "Every inch."

He pushed her against the bed with a soft press of his large hand against her chest. She lay still as she studied him, seemingly anticipating what he would do to her. He wasn't sure what he would do. He wanted to do it all, soft sweet things, and dirty filthy things too. And her expression told him that she would let him. But mostly, he wanted to stamp her into his brain. This would be their last time together. She had said as much. *'One last time.'*

He trailed his finger along the delicate lace of her brassiere and drew lazy circles around her hardened nipple, clearly visible through the see-through fabric. Damn if that wasn't the sweetest, most perfect nipple he had ever seen. He wanted to bite it. But he restrained himself, and stroked it with the tip of his finger instead. She let out a soft cry, and he loved it. He was teasing her, and he had never had so much fun.

He smiled playfully at her as he realized he had two hands to use, to pleasure her with. He trailed his other hand to the band of her panties, stroking the soft skin above, playing with her. She lifted her hips slightly off the bed and reached for him.

"Not yet," he whispered. "This is about you. I want to make you come."

She closed her eyes and threw her head back. "God..."

With other women, it had always been a given that he would pleasure them. He was a gentleman, after all. And their pleasure was as important as his, if not even more so. But with them, he was rather just going through the motions, not really taking them in. They were really all the same to him, beautiful curves, and soft warm flesh.

But with Kirsten, it was different. He actually craved her pleasure intensely. He reveled in her little moans, he got off when she melted into him, became unhinged, lost her senses under his touch. Every moan, every sweet breath aroused him, made him harder, made his body ache for her. It was a feast, seeing this proper little thing become someone else under his spell.

He slipped a finger under the lace, gently pulling at her panties. This was obviously not all about getting off. It was also about making sure she would come, because once he was inside her, he wasn't sure how long he could last. Suddenly, it was like he was sixteen again.

She squirmed as he pulled off her panties and trailed kisses along her curves and the soft curls down below. He wanted to taste and he was going to, as soon as he got her undies off and her legs wrapped around his head.

"Ethan..." she called out his name in a long breath when his mouth landed on her sex. He licked softly at first, taking her in. She tasted as sweet as candy. She wailed and moaned, almost as if she was in pain. But he knew he wasn't hurting her. He was being tender.

"H-harder," she cried out, the word all broken up.

He parted her lips with a finger and glided his tongue hard against her clit, eliciting a loud groan. He loved that she was enjoying this so much. And as he went harder and faster at her, she wiggled and pressed herself against him. He dug his hands into her sweet little rear as he went at her like she was his last meal. She moaned and wailed herself into a frenzy, pulling at his hair. He stole one or two looks at her because he wanted to see... everything. She was beautiful. Her moans and breathing grew in intensity and she finally cried out when she came. Damn, little Miss Librarian was wild.

He pulled himself to her, her taste still on his mouth. She looked spent, satiated. She opened her eyes slowly to look at him. "God, you are good at that."

He smiled wide, rather proud of himself. "Thanks... I loved it too."

God, he was breathtaking, leaning over her, completely naked. She trailed the tips of her fingers over his chest and sculpted abs, the skin so perfect and smooth. He flashed her a wicked grin, a spark in his eyes. He obviously wasn't quite done with her. But all she wanted to do at that moment was take him in, admire him. Her hand traveled lower. He was still big and hard for her. She reveled in the warmth of him and inched her body over his. She slithered down to take him in her mouth. He groaned loudly as she took him deeper. But as she twirled her tongue around him, she felt him tense. She didn't have too much experience in this department but she knew enough to know what makes a man tic. He pulled at her arm and brought her to him. His mouth pressed gently against hers. "I want to be inside you."

Damn, she wanted that so much too. He reached around and unclasped her brassiere with ease, and then he peeled off the delicate straps off of her shoulder with a gentleness she had never experienced before. He was handling her like a fragile priceless piece of art. As her bra fell to the mattress, he took her breast in his mouth and the heat of his tongue coursed through her. She never wanted this to end. She liked it like this, slow and tender. She couldn't remember the last time she had been made love to like this, with such emotion and sweetness.

She wanted to kiss him again. She craved his mouth, the taste of him. She pulled him to her and she took possession of him, her tongue and his, melting into one another, her taste still on his lips. His erection pressed again her and she could feel him lose himself. He pulled away reluctantly, a pained expression on his face. "I need to go get—"

"It's okay," she told him. "I'm on the pill." She had always been on the pill. She had never gone off it. But now, she trusted him. Although she was fully aware of his reputation, she knew he was smart about his affairs and he would never jeopardize her health and well-being. She trusted him.

His eyes darkened when he asked her, "Are you sure?"

"I trust you," she told him. "I know you would never hurt me."

"I wouldn't," he agreed. "I'm always very careful. I never..." he tried to explain. "But with you, I can..."

She pulled him to her and kissed him again. His hands traveled through her hair, and his mouth took her with hunger. She felt a tinge of pain as he held her bottom lip hostage between his teeth, but she loved it. She reached for him, guided him to the wetness between her thighs, craving him so desperately. He let out a long sigh as he sank into her. She pressed herself hard against him and tangled her legs around him. He felt so good, she never wanted to let go. As he pressed into her repeatedly, hard and slow, she could sense her body tensing. He was going to make her come again. His mouth left hers and his breath was ragged, all over the place. He closed his eyes, seemingly struggling. "God, you feel so good. I don't know if I can—"

"Let go," she whispered. She wanted to feel him completely, feel the strength and passion in him. He threw his head against the hollow at the base of her neck and grabbed her hips with such fierceness, he took her by surprise. And he pressed harder, deeper and pounded into her hard, the headboard bounced off the wall. It was so good, Kirsten knew she would soon fall over the edge too. As he pushed her so hard, he hurt her but also brought out her climax which had been building ever sense he had penetrated her. As the waves of pleasure consumed her whole body, she felt him still and groan into the flesh of her shoulder.

He pulled away from her slowly. With the weight of his body off her, she suddenly felt cold and empty. She wanted him close again. Almost as if he could read her mind, he grabbed the fluffy comforter, wrapped his arm around her and pulled her to him. Side by side, huddled under the soft weight of the designer silk bed cover, she might as well have been laying on a cloud. She felt so complete. "That was amazing," he whispered against her ear.

"It was..." Sex. Making love. Whatever this was, it couldn't be beat. Sadness washed over her as she remembered they couldn't keep doing this. This had been their last time. *One last time'*, she had told him. And he had nodded in full agreement.

"I loved every second of it," he told her. "But I also love just laying here with you like this."

She smiled. "Me too."

Silence filled the room but it wasn't uncomfortable or awkward. "Thank you," she said, her words soft. "You've made me forget all about Logan."

The problem was now she'd have to forget all about Ethan, and although they hadn't spent five years together, she had a feeling it would be even harder. She didn't quite understand it. It was crazy.

"The guy sounds like a jerk. He's not worth even a second of your time. I'm glad I could be of assistance."

"I've pretty much forgotten all about him, which is crazy because we were together five years."

His fingers trailed softly along the curve of her hip. "You probably didn't really love him."

"And he obviously didn't love me," she pointed out. "The jerk broke up with me on the Great Wheel, of all places."

Ethan looked at her, wide-eyed. "He did?"

"Well, it all started there, when I realized we weren't getting engaged and that something was up. I was on the verge of tears when I got off the gondola car," she went on. "But he did the official deed at a little crêperie shop, and told me he was in love with a yoga instructor."

"That's weak," Ethan said. "What an asshole."

"I can't even look at that wheel anymore," she confessed. "Too many bad memories."

He laughed. "That must be hard," he said. "She's pretty hard to miss."

"Tell me about it."

As he stroked her arm softly, she felt her lids getting heavier, her thoughts getting hazier. The green numbers on his digital clock indicated 3:12 AM. She was exhausted. She pressed closer to him and let herself drift away. As much as she wanted the night to last forever, she knew it couldn't.

9

———

SORRY, I NEVER MAKE MY BED

He took in every inch of her as she slept, the long dark lashes, the delicate nose, the hint of a smile as she slumbered, hand tucked delicately under one cheek. She slept like a princess. He had been told, that he himself, slept like an ogre, on his back, mouth opened, snoring up a storm. But she... she looked like a sweet little doll. He wanted to wake her with a naughty lick or bite but he also wanted to watch her sleep forever. He was torn. On the one hand, the longer she slept, the longer he would have her in his bed. But on the other, he had this raging erection, and he really wanted to have her again. But they had both agreed. *One last time.* Did that mean this was it? Or was this morning included in the whole deal?

A morning erection is a powerful thing, powerful enough to affect someone's common sense. He had none when he pressed his lips against the curve of her hip, tasting the slightly salty skin. He pressed her flat on the bed, and his tongue traveled around her navel and below. He felt her stir and heard her moan, and realized he had woken her. But he couldn't help himself. He glanced at her and spotted a smile on her face. She was game. His little dragonfly was all in for a little morning glory.

He traveled up her body and kissed her neck. When he got too close, she turned away from him. "I have morning breath," she mumbled. But by the way she turned and stretched her arms long above her head, propped her rear against him, her beautiful back on full display, he knew she wanted to play. She shivered as he dragged a finger along her spine, from the top of her delicate neck, all the way down to the tip of her ass crack. He grabbed her hips and lifted her bottom against his hips. She held herself at an odd angle and eased him into her, a delicious grin on her face. She was enjoying every second. He stroked her clit gently with a soft hand as he pushed into her. As the sensation hit him harder and he could sense her getting wilder and closer, he pushed harder and stroked faster until he heard the familiar moans of pleasure. And he soon lost himself in it too.

Spent, he pulled her to him. In complete contrast to last night's love making, this had been a quickie. No kisses, no tenderness, purely for the physical pleasure of it. And that was okay too. He loved bringing her pleasure. In a perfect world, he would love to do it every day, morning, noon and night. But he knew they were not meant to be together. They were too different. She was a traditionalist, a good girl who wanted marriage, kids, and a white picket fence, and he had vowed to never ever get married. He was a player, and he'd always owned that.

But somehow, something had changed lately. He hadn't been with another woman since that Boeuf Bourguignon dinner, and this was completely unusual for him.

"So technically," Kirsten started, "we said 'one last time' but that was two."

He pressed a smile against the back of her shoulder. "We've been pretty naughty."

She laughed, the sound soft. "I like being naughty."

He smiled. She was so sweet. "I've noticed."

"I meant what I said though," she went on, her tone serious. "This has to be officially over between us now. You could really break my heart, you know. If we got too involved... if I got too attached."

"You're right," he conceded as much as he didn't want to. "I agree it's probably for the best. We could be friends."

He felt her stiffen and pull from him. "I don't think that would work, Ethan," she argued. "I think we should just be civil, say hi if we happen to run into each other, which is likely to happen. And that's it."

A weight pressed on his chest. It was a foreign sensation. How could she be so pragmatic about it? Did she not care about him too? Or was this just a 'girl gone wild' kind of thing? He knew she didn't take a man like him seriously. She was looking for a serious, conservative, no-nonsense kind of guy. But what about Cole? He didn't quite fit that description either.

"Why aren't you in Cole's bed this morning?" he asked, daring to go there. "Why are you in mine? You two seemed to be hitting it off last night."

She smiled at him as she pulled her panties back on. "We just met," she explained. "I can't just jump into the man's bed. That's one of your rules, Mr. Fox, if you'll recall."

"So I see," he scoffed. The thought of her with Cole drove him wild. "So he gets you nice and wet, and then you come to me to get fucked good and hard. Because I don't matter, do I?"

She jerked her head back, mouth opened. "For your information, yes... the guy's gorgeous, but if anyone got me nice and wet last night, it was you. I wish it were him, but it was you."

Her words aroused him so much, he couldn't think straight. He was left speechless as she carried on. "You're the only one who has this effect on me, who makes me want to forget everything, and just get lost..."

"I feel the same way," he tried to explain. Did he ever. But she wouldn't listen. She grabbed her bra and robe and scurried off.

"We're doing it again," she pointed out as she put her robe back on. "Let's just stop it. Okay? Let's just stop talking."

And with those words, she made her way to the front door and left him standing there, naked and confused.

He had dismissed her so easily when she had told him she wanted to end things. She wished he had fought her a little harder. 'We could be friends'. What kind of bull crap was that? She highly doubted that they could remain friends after everything they'd shared. Two people cannot make love like they did last night, and be 'friends'. She tip-toed to her room, not wanting her mother to notice her coming in at this hour. But unfortunately, Lorraine was already up, nursing a cup of coffee and doing her crossword puzzle. Damn her and her early bird ways.

Lorraine flashed her the hugest grin she had ever seen. Kirsten bit her bottom lip, her sexy bra still in her hand, all the evidence her mother needed.

"Yes, it is exactly what it looks like," she conceded.

Lorraine smiled. "Curious," she started and Kirsten knew she was in for another one of her playful little talks. Her mother got off on drama, which was probably one of the reasons she was a romance writer. "So... you and Cole seem to have had yourselves a good time last night. But yet... here you are in your bath robe. You are clearly not coming back from his place. You would be wearing last night's little blue dress."

"Congratulations, Sherlock," Kirsten smirked. "You've solved the mystery."

"Why are you sleeping with Ethan?" her mother asked with an expression of concern. "I thought you hated him. And here you were yesterday, hitting it off with the most delicious man I've ever seen."

Kirsten slumped herself on the kitchen chair, across from her mother. "I don't know," she confessed. "I know it's crazy, but he's all I can think about... he's under my skin."

Lorraine nodded and pulled her chair closer to her daughter. She wrapped an arm around her. And Kirsten couldn't rein in her emotions anymore. She let the tears flow in the comfort of her mother's security. Lorraine went on, "It has always fascinated me," she told her daughter, "...love."

Kirsten wiped her nose with the sleeve of her robe, listening.

"I think that's why I write romance," Lorraine carried on. "It's crazy how stubborn the heart is. Here you have two guys. One is beautiful, kind and right for you, and the other is all wrong. Yet, he's the one you want, the one you crave."

Kirsten nodded with a hint of a smile. That's exactly how it was. Her mother was a master, a real love guru. "It's so annoying."

"You tell me," Lorraine smirked. "I've been there." She held her closer, patting her head. "Can I make you waffles with blueberries and fresh cream?" she ventured. "It's your favorite."

That did sound pretty good. Her mother did not cook very much, but she was a master with that waffle maker... and J-Ello.

She smiled at her mother. "Sure." Perhaps a little whipped cream could ease the pain. As far as Kirsten knew, whipped cream always made everything better.

She was certainly doing quite the number on him. He had never been so shaken up by a woman before. It was time to take the bull by the horn and take control of his life. Where was the old Ethan Fox? The ladies' man had gone AWOL. And it was time to find him, and forget all about Kirsten Beals. He pondered his options as he made himself a strawberry-banana whey powder smoothie. He could consult his 'little black book', also known as his cell: phone contacts and social media contacts. All he had to do was spend a half-hour and send a few messages.

But he didn't really want to dig into his past affairs. They wouldn't help him forget. None of them measured up to Kirsten. He needed someone new. It would be easy enough, he thought as he lounged on his sectional. It was just a matter of dressing up and going to his favorite club, flashing a smile or two, buying a girl a drink.

All he knew was that he desperately needed to do something. As soon as possible.

KIRSTEN WAS surprised when the white tulips were delivered. For a fraction of a second, she had hoped they were from Ethan. But she knew better. They had both agreed to end things. She was only a little disappointed when she read the card and realized they were from Cole, and a part of her was happy, touched... He was such a gentleman. The bouquet was simple and the vase was very interesting. It appeared to be recycled from tree materials. She centered it on the kitchen table, all the while smiling like an idiot.

"My, my, my..." her mother quipped. "Someone is smitten."

"Aren't they lovely?"

"Beautiful," her mother agreed, reading the small white card. "I'm not crazy about the vase though. Doesn't quite fit in with my décor."

"You're not touching it, Mother."

They both laughed. "Do you have another date?"

"I'm not sure," she told her mother. "I'll call him to thank him. And I'm sure we'll set something up. This is just what I need right now."

"I'm happy for you, sweetie."

Me too, Kirsten thought. Perhaps she was *finally* on the right track.

ETHAN NURSED a scotch as he sat at the bar. He didn't want to be there. For the first time in recent years, he was not looking forward to the thrill of the chase. And often it didn't feel much like a chase. He felt rather like the prey. Woman these days were so sexually adventurous and independent. They knew exactly what they wanted, and often that would be his 'services'. He had acquired a certain set of 'skills' which suited him well when it came to seducing the ladies. He'd always enjoyed the buzz of the night, the excitement and anticipation, the mystery of who he would take home.

But tonight, he might as well have been reading a quarterly report. It wasn't a lack of beautiful women. The place was packed and everyone was looking as fine as ever. This particular club catered to the well-off, and often very beautiful people. The drinks were crazy expensive but the ambiance was worth it.

Despite being surrounded by beautiful women, all he could think about was Kirsten. Her sweet smile, her insanely beautiful eyes, and that hair. Her little mannerisms clouded his brain, how she would snort a little when she laughed hard, or how she straightened her shoulders and threw her nose up when she was angry. And the sounds she made when she came under his touch. He couldn't even go there, lest he drive himself crazy.

He shook his head and spotted a gorgeous woman to his left. She shot him a perfect smile as soon as he made eye contact. She was absolute perfection, exactly the type of woman he'd usually be all over in less than a second. She was alone, sipping a green cocktail. She tilted her head and shot him a look, and then pulled her gaze away. And then again. She was flirting, without a word. Ethan knew this but he wasn't sure he wanted to take the bait. He couldn't help but wonder what the hell was going on with him. He was acting like an idiot as far as he was concerned. Here was this gorgeous babe who was clearly interested, and he was *hesitating.*

So he did what he did best. He slid over and closed the distance between them. He noticed her cocktail was low. He flashed her his charismatic smile. "Can I buy you another?" he asked. "What will you have?"

She smiled wide. "I wouldn't mind another appletini."

"Done," he said with a lingering gaze. She was here alone and dressed like a high-end escort. He was sure she wasn't. There was something about her... She lacked the cockiness, the all-business manner. She was beautiful and charming, but she was no pro. "I'm Ethan, by the way."

She extended her manicured hand. "I'm Natasha."

He smiled. "It's nice to meet you, Natasha," he offered. "That's a beautiful name." Admittedly, he was not at his most original, but he was a little uninspired. Nevertheless, it seemed to work. It was so easy.

She grinned like a school girl. "Thank you."

She had an exotic look about her, which he very much liked. "What's the story behind your name?" he asked. This question was always a good ice-breaker.

She laughed. "I'm not sure there is a story," she told him. "My mother just liked the name, I suppose. I don't think it's a traditional Columbian name," she went on. "My mother is Columbian."

"That's cool," he offered. "So have you ever been to Columbia?" Ethan had been many places but never to Columbia. He was genuinely fascinated. He loved learning about new cultures and countries.

And so the conversation started, flowing smoothly. He found Natasha not only beautiful, but also intelligent and occasionally funny. As he ordered her another drink, he concluded that she might be the perfect woman to help him forget all about Kirsten Beals.

Kirsten's week was not starting off on the right track. She was swamped with work. On the one hand, it was good to keep busy. Less time to think about Ethan. But on the other, she was overwhelmed. Not only did she have to do her regular duties, but she also had to wrinkle out some details and odds and ends for the upcoming fundraiser for the library.

She dreaded the event. She would see Logan there and she really didn't want to. Funny enough though, he had barely entered her mind these past few weeks. Her thoughts had been consumed by Ethan. She had, in essence, filled the hole in her heart with Ethan, and now she was trying to fill the hole caused by Ethan with Cole.

As she shuffled some papers around, she adjusted her glasses and gazed into the distance. The stacks of books became a blurry rainbow of colors. She pondered her situation. Perhaps, she should just be alone for a while and not try to replace anybody with anyone else, she mused. She contemplated being on her own for a while, independent. Starting something with Cole might be just the worst thing she could do right now, she realized – she wasn't in the right state of mind to start a new relationship – she had to completely get over Ethan before she could do that.

Besides, she had absolutely no time for men at this moment. She would be working extra hours for the next week or two. And just the thought of dating exhausted her. She would be better off with a bowl of popcorn and *Gilmore Girls*, not more drama. Fictional TV drama. Yes. But real-life drama. No. She'd had enough of that lately.

And perhaps, she would work on her current writing project, her modern day retelling of Jane's Austen's *Pride and Prejudice*.

ETHAN WORKED OUT HIS STRESS, really going hard at the gym. He was trying the keep his thoughts at bay. Work, Natasha, Kirsten... especially Kirsten. He was going out with Natasha tonight and he was working off some nervous energy. Part of him didn't really want to go out with Natasha, but he knew it was what he had to do. Some meaningless casual sex might just do the trick.

COLE AND KIRSTEN met up at a quaint coffee shop near his place. Over lattés, they talked about their jobs, their passions, and... life. He was so easy to talk to. She told him all about her retelling of Jane Austen. He seemed intrigued. He told her all about a modern art exposition he was participating in, coming up in two weeks, and she promised she'd be there. They also discussed art and literature. They had so much in common, it was surprising. She told him all about Logan, and he'd shared his own recent break-up. It seemed, they were both trying to get over people. He asked her about Ethan. He remembered him from the gastro pub.

"So you two ever had a thing?" he asked, curious.

"Uh..." she hesitated a bit. How much should she tell him? She decided to downplay it. "He's just my next door neighbor, some tech wiz. He's a little arrogant."

Cole smiled, and she couldn't help but notice he had a very nice smile. "Yep, I kind of got that impression."

She laughed. "That obvious?"

His face grew serious. "I'm surprised he's just a neighbor. For some reason, I thought he was an old boyfriend. I kind of got that vibe."

"What would make you say that?"

He shrugged. "I don't know... the energy between you two."

Energy. That was oddly enough, an appropriate word to describe their relationship, Kirsten mused. It seemed they both lit up when they saw each other. And the sex was electric. She sighed, trying to forget him. Why were they talking about Ethan Fox?

"So tell me all about your work," she said, desperately wanting to change the subject. "Do you work from your loft?"

"Yep," he told her, a spark in his eyes. She could tell he was one of those rare lucky people who get to do what they love every day. "I have a pretty large space," he went on. "It's mostly studio. The kitchen is small and the living area is practically non-existent, and my bed is tucked in a corner."

"It must be a mess," she chimed in with a hint of a smile. "I can only imagine."

He laughed. "Yes... it's pretty crazy," he confessed. "But I try to be organized, 'try' being the operative word here."

She laughed. She enjoyed this casual chit chat. The dynamic between them was wonderful. No drama. No games. "What are you working on at the moment?"

"I'm working on a series for a building downtown, which houses a bunch of tech companies," he told her. "It's a series of eight pieces, and the theme is nature coming together with technology, and how it is possible for the two to be harmonious."

Kirsten was impressed, listening to him. He seemed so passionate. She tried to picture his sculptures and she was at a loss. "What medium to you work with?"

"Mostly wire and metal," he replied. "My style is very distinct. No one is doing quite what I'm doing at the moment. I think that's why I've had success."

"That and the fact that you're probably crazy talented."

He smiled at her wide. "I could show you."

"Show me?"

"Yes, if you have time," he ventured, looking a little on edge. "You could come to my studio. I could show you what I'm currently working on."

Kirsten was quite excited at the prospect of visiting his studio, but part of her thought it might be a little too early in their relationship to be going to his place. They hadn't even kissed yet. And she had decided she would rather just remain friends for the moment, and not get involved with anyone. "Well, I don't know..." she hesitated, an internal struggle weighing on her. She really wanted to go.

"C'mon," he insisted. "It'll be fun."

She was acting too uptight again. She had promised herself she would try to loosen up a little. "Sure, why not," she finally agreed.

Cole's studio was crazy cool, lots of light coming from both the large floor-to-ceiling garage door windows and overhanging light fixtures. The whole space had a very industrial vibe. "This is amazing," she offered, wide-eyed. She couldn't help but think that Cole was cool with a capital C.

"Thanks... it's an old converted mechanics garage. Which is why it's so grungy."

She laughed, eyeing the large wire and metal sculpture smack in the middle of the space. A tree, surrounded by rings. It was quite beautiful.

"It works for me," he went on, walking leisurely through the space. "It's easy to move around the sculptures, being on ground level like this with large garage door access. The moving van can pull directly up."

She studied the door, the overcast sky reflecting in. "Don't you lack privacy?" she asked. She couldn't imagine living like this, so open to the world. She enjoyed being on the 22nd floor in a loft building, sheltered from others.

He reached to the side, pulled on a loop of thick rope, and large heavy black curtains slid across the doors, transforming the space from bright and airy to dark, and dungeon-y.

She smiled. "Cool."

He grabbed her hand. "Come," he urged. "I'll give you the grand tour."

She laughed. "I think I can see everything from right here." And she could. From where she was standing, she could see the tiny kitchen with its old 1970s appliances, and the cozy living area furnished with what looked like flea market finds. The overall effect was very warm.

"You make a good point," he conceded. "So that is the kitchen and living room. And here," he added as he pulled her to the nook tucked in at the back, "is the bathroom and bedroom."

She peeked in the bathroom, a small space with a very old-looking shower and claw-footed tub. This was no fancy reproduction, but the real thing. Subway tiles covered the walls and gave the cozy space a vintage feel. "I like it."

And she turned to see the disheveled queen size mattress on the floor covered with white linens.

"Sorry, I never make my bed," he admitted.

"We're very different, you and I," she pointed out. "I always make my bed."

He shot her a playful smile. "Oh... you're one of those," he teased. "I see..."

He had inched nearer and was closing in on her, two gorgeous steely-blue eyes honing in on her. She knew that look. Dark cozy space, privacy, unmade bed. A man and a woman.

She knew exactly what he was thinking.

10
————

I FEEL LIKE DOING SOMETHING CRAZY

"You can make my bed, if the sight of it is you crazy," Cole teased as he pressed the palm of his hand against her jawline, tilting her head to his. The man was truly beautiful and impossibly sexy. Any woman would practically kill to be standing where she was right now.

But she wasn't feeling it... at all. What was wrong with her? She had vowed to be more wild and free, but she was failing miserably. Perhaps, she just needed a bit more time. Perhaps he was moving a little too fast. They hadn't even kissed yet, and he was clearly thinking about sex. But then again, she and Ethan had never even kissed when they first had sex, and he had taken her from behind on the back of a sofa in a fevered quickie, but somehow, even that felt less gratuitous than this. Cole pressed his lips against hers. She closed her eyes as he coaxed her tongue with his. He pressed his arms closer around her, pulling her in.

She tore away gently, and he released her with an expression of complete confusion. Cole didn't seem like the kind of man who got rejected often, which was probably why he looked so shocked. "I'm sorry," she offered. "It's just... this is all moving a little too fast."

He backed away. "I see..."

"It's not that I don't like you," she tried to explain. "It's just that I just got out of a serious long-term relationship, and I'm not quite ready."

He nodded but she could see the disappointment on his face. "I understand," he said. "I just got out of a relationship too."

"I just think we should take it slowly," she went on. "I don't want you to be a rebound." She now knew from experience that rebound flings were never a good idea. A person is way too emotional and vulnerable after a break-up.

"If I give you a little more time," he ventured softly. "You think you and I..."

She smiled at him. "Definitely."

"Then I can wait. I really like you, Kirsten."

He was so sweet. Why wasn't she crazy about him yet? "You know what..." She suddenly remembered. "I have a fundraiser in a few weeks, and I'm still looking for a date," she told him. "Would you be interested?"

He smiled wide, grabbing her hand. "I would love to."

He led her back to the central studio space. And she admired his work-in-progress again. "This is truly beautiful. It looks done."

"It almost is," he told her. "Just a few finishing touches. I'm a perfectionist."

She smiled. "Me too."

ETHAN STUDIED Natasha as she fiddled, searching for something in her bejeweled clutch. She pulled out a lip gloss and applied it meticulously, all the while staring at him with an expression that could only be read as *I'm a siren of seduction, and I know it.* She knew exactly what she was doing. She was also perfection, long hair meticulously styled, manicured red-tipped fingers, a designer curve-hugging red dress, a few inches shorter than appropriate.

She was the kind of woman he'd normally have in his bed before ten o'clock. But there was something about her that was different. She had a little more class than most and he, for some reason, suspected that she would never sleep with him on the first date. And oddly enough, he wasn't irked by this fact. He was fine with it. He preferred to wait too.

As pleasant as she was, he did not feel that spark, that energy, that stomach churning anticipation he'd always felt when he was with Kirsten. Kirsten... He really had to forget about her.

They made small-talk as they enjoyed their meals; filet mignon for him and shrimp and pasta for her. She was clearly very smart. She'd been an English lit major at Stanford. And her family was well off. Her parents had made a fortune in telecommunications in the late 90s. When she spoke of her family, her eyes lit up, and Ethan imagined he'd get along just fine with her father. This was the kind of woman he should have been looking to settle down with, the kind of woman his father would approve of. She would be the perfect wife, the perfect mother.

But the thing was... She didn't stir him up. And how would that hold up in a life-long marriage? Because for Ethan, marriage wasn't something you took lightly. If he ever chose to get married, he'd be in it for the long haul. For that reason, he had to choose wisely. And despite the fact that he had always told himself he would never settle down, he was actually getting a little bored with the clubbing scene. All the women started to look and sound like each other. They had truly become interchangeable.

As he drove Natasha back to her place, he could only think of Kirsten. What was she doing? Was she with Cole? How serious were those two? Had they had sex yet? He grasped the steering wheel hard. The thought made him slightly angry. But then he told himself it's what he wanted for her. He wanted her to go out there and discover her sexuality, apply what he'd taught her, not that he'd taught her very much. He wanted her to be free and wild. Because after all, she truly was a friend. And he wanted her to be happy.

But what he had to work on now, he thought as he flashed Natasha a smile, was his own happiness. And the first step toward that goal was forgetting all about Kirsten Beals.

He walked Natasha to the from door of her apartment building, a posh complex surrounded by an attractive landscaped courtyard.

"I had a great time," she told him with a wide smile and he could tell she was being genuine.

"Me too." He hadn't succeeded in forgetting about Kirsten, but the evening had been pleasant. "Let's do it again sometime."

"Definitely," she agreed. And she stood awkwardly for a beat or two. "I'd invite you in, but I need to get to bed. I've got an early flight tomorrow morning."

"Oh yes... Hawaii." She had told him all about the trip she was taking with her family; her parents and siblings.

"I'll call you when I get back, and maybe we could go out again."

"Two whole weeks," he pointed out. "I may very well go crazy waiting."

She laughed, a soft giggle. "That's sweet."

He hadn't meant to be sweet. He was in fact, going to go crazy, with no one to keep his mind off Kirsten.

He inched closer and kissed her on the cheek, a very gentleman move. He knew it was the right play. She was being demure, making him wait a little, making him desire her, giving him the thrill of the chase. Unlike Kirsten, Natasha knew exactly how this game was played. She smiled at him one last time and slipped into her apartment building. As she walked out of sight, she waved good-bye. He blew her a kiss, wishing he could just go to bed and sleep for two weeks.

KIRSTEN WAS TRYING to read a book, a classic, one of her favorites. But she just couldn't focus. She'd read the same paragraph three times now. She slammed the book closed, shut her eyes and stretched across the sofa. She thought about him. She'd promise herself she wouldn't. Just this once, she would indulge in thoughts of him.

She thought about the night they made love, how every touch, every kiss had sent a current through her, lit her up. She desperately wanted to feel that again, but she doubted if any man would ever be able to help her achieve that ever again. She couldn't imagine wanting anyone as much as she wanted Ethan. Her whole body ached for him.

She smothered her face with one of the fluffy feathery cushions on her mother's sofa. She realized she was going insane. She desperately needed to do something about this. She picked up her phone and reviewed the texts Cole had left her. Nothing crazy, just a few friendly hellos. She hadn't replied. After the incident at his place, she was a little gun shy about getting too involved with him. She knew what he wanted and she wasn't sure she was quite ready for that yet.

But it was Saturday night and she desperately needed the distraction. She bit her bottom lip as she waited for him to answer.

"Hey."

"Hi," she replied, feeling a little nervous.

"What's up?"

"Not much," she told him. "Listen, I got your texts. I've just been swamped."

"No worries," he told her. "I know how it is."

"Good, I'm glad," she said. "So... anyway," she went on, hesitating for a beat or two. "I was wondering what you were up to tonight."

"Me and my buddy are going to a party," he told her and her heart sank at his words. She'd wanted to spend some time with him and do something fun, get her mind off things, namely off thoughts of herself naked with a certain Mr. Fox.

"Oh... cool," she said, at a loss for words. What was she going to do now? Binge watch *Gilmore Girls*?

"You could come with us if you'd like," he suggested. "It's this cool guy we know who lives in Georgetown. He does this every year. There's Blackjack and Poker... it's a casino party."

Kirsten perked up. That did sound like a lot of fun. "Isn't that illegal?" she couldn't help but ask. The words slipped out before she could catch herself.

He laughed. "Well, let's not tell anyone, okay?"

"My lips are sealed."

"So are you interested in tagging along?"

"Are you sure?" she asked. "It kind of sounds like a guys' thing. You probably don't want a woman cramping your style."

"No... seriously, Kirsten," he insisted. "I'd really like you to come. I actually thought of calling you up but I didn't want to be too pushy, since you hadn't returned my texts."

"I'm sorry about that," she apologized again. "Yes... I'd love to come. Can you pick me up?"

"Yep, I can," he told her and she could almost hear the happiness in his voice. "We'll meet my buddy Chris at the party."

"Sounds good."

Kirsten couldn't figure out what to wear. She had never been to a casino party in Georgetown. She would be surrounded by strangers and she was sure she would probably cling to Cole. She thought about Cole and what his friends might be like. She had met Max, obviously. But she was under the impression that Max wasn't a typical friend. Max was a high-finance guy who collected art. She was sure his other friends were quite different. She pictured them dressed in black, sporting tattoos and body piercings like Cole did.

She finally settled on a little black dress, and she decided to pair it up with her worn brown riding boots, which she used to wear when she hiked with Logan. As she applied her makeup and styled her hair, she decided to go for bombshell sexy, like the night Meghan had made her up, the night she first had sex with Ethan.

And there she was, thinking about him again. This happened so often, it was excruciating. The worst part was that she knew he was right next door, and that she could easily become undone and walk right up to his door. She was surprised she hadn't done it yet. She had had amazing willpower. Because numerous times a day, she would think about him, her body would swell with desire and she ached to reach out to him. But she didn't want to be that woman, desperate, clingy, and wild. She was better than that.

She picked up the phone and dialed, her fingers shaking.

Meghan answered on the third ring. Kirsten was nervous making the first move. But she had really liked Meghan and the two of them had gotten along famously. A girlfriend could do her good, occupy her mind, even if that girlfriend just so happened to be a Fox too.

"Hi, Meghan," she ventured. "How are you?"

"Hi, Kirsten," Meghan cheered, clearly glad to hear from her. "I'm so happy to hear from you. I was actually thinking about calling you."

"I was just doing my hair and makeup," Kirsten told her. "And it made me think of you."

"Are you going out?"

"Yep... to some party with this guy I'm seeing."

"Oh..." Meghan trailed off.

"What?"

"Oh... it's just that I kind of thought you were seeing my brother," she clarified. "You're all he talks about."

Kirsten's breath hitched at Meghan's words. "Oh..."

"And I was under the impression that you two... you know... that night I gave you the makeover."

Kirsten blushed. "Well... sort of," she confessed. "But he and I are too different."

She laughed, a soft chuckle. "I know he can be quite the Casanova, but lately, he's been different."

"Really?" Kirsten asked, intrigued.

"Well, anyway, listen... you and I should get together for lunch sometime soon."

Kirsten perked up. "I'd like that."

"I don't work too far from you," Meghan went on. "And I know this great little Vietnamese place and they have the best bubble tea. You like bubble tea?"

Kirsten smiled. "I've never had it, but it does sound fun."

"It's a date then," Meghan cheered. "I'll text you the details."

Kirsten smiled as she pressed on *end call*. Perhaps something good could come out of all this, after all. A new friendship. She studied her reflection one last time, satisfied with the results. Very rock-chick cool.

As she made her way to the lobby, she was filled with energy, anticipating a fun night. Cole was stretched across the lobby sofa, looking delicious. Yes... 'delicious' was definitely an apt word to describe him. He did a double-take when he spotted her. "You look... different," he said as he stood to meet her. "You look amazing."

"Thanks," she said, taking in his worn leather jacket and the motorcycle helmet hanging off his hand. "Uh... you came here on a bike."

He flashed her a wide grin. "Yep... didn't you notice it in my driveway when you were at my place?"

"No..." Was he expecting her to ride on his bike? She had never ridden on a motorcycle before. She was ill-equipped to do so, wearing a short dress, no jacket, and no helmet. There was no way she was going on that thing without a helmet.

He smiled wide as he grabbed her hand. "You look terrified. I'll ride safely... there's nothing to worry about."

"But..." Kirsten tried to object.

He handed her the helmet and peeled off his jacket as they made their way to the shiny Harley. It was a beauty. "Here, you can have my jacket too."

"Are you sure?"

He helped her into the jacket which hung off her. He laughed. "God... you are tiny."

She scowled at him. She much preferred the term 'petite'. "And this thing..." she ventured, still holding on to the helmet.

He grabbed it and adjusted it just so on her head. The sensation of it was odd... foreign.

She wrapped her arms tightly around his torso as they sped off into the Seattle night. She felt a rush as they headed toward Georgetown. The speed, the wind, the thrill... it was all so cool.

The party was exactly as she expected. Ultra cool tattooed hipsters, and Goth girls with vintage Doc Martens and way too much eye makeup. Kirsten stood out, but just a little. A nose ring and arm tattoo, and she'd fit in seamlessly. Foreign beer seemed to be the drink of choice. She craved a cocktail but there didn't seem too much of those going around. She wondered where the bar was.

The music was good, a mix of alternative indie rock and remakes of old 80s songs. She was quite familiar with all the old 80s songs because she had been listening to them all her life with her mom. Duran Duran, The Thompson Twins and The Cure were favorites of Lorraine's.

Cole rested a hand on the small of her back as he lead her through the crowd huddled in the small industrial loft space. He introduced her to a bunch of people, whose names she promptly forgot despite herself. There were just too many people, too much stimulation. A blackjack table and two poker tables were set up, and the smell of marijuana smoke permeated the air. She didn't particularly want to partake but she couldn't help but think that this was the coolest party she'd ever been to. Mind you, she hadn't been to many.

Cole fetched her a gin and tonic and a few hours later, she was on her third one, feeling pretty good and kicking ass at the blackjack table. She'd always loved the game. She'd played it often with Lorraine. Feeling nostalgic, she appreciated the fact that she hadn't had a standard childhood. Hers had been filled with 80s music, mani-pedis, books, blackjack and cards, waffles for dinner, trips to the beach, shopping, and dancing in the living room.

She was feeling light and smooth as Cole rubbed her shoulders and dug his fingers into her hair. "You want to get out of here?"

She turned to him, wanting to ride on his bike into the night, to be wild and free again. She wondered if he had drunk too much. "Are you okay to drive?"

He smiled. "Always. I don't drink."

She stared at him, wide-eyed. "Why?"

"Well, let's just say I drank a little too much when I was younger, and I discovered it was all or nothing for me," he told her as he wrapped his jacket around her shoulders. "Well, when it comes to alcohol and drugs, anyway..." he added, and with a pensive expression, he said, "and with relationships too, I suppose."

All or nothing. That's how she was too. No casual flings. No 'friends with benefits' arrangements. She wanted to be 'all in'. She supposed that was the reason it had been so hard with Ethan. He didn't want either all or nothing. He was happy somewhere in the middle.

They hopped on the bike and flew off into the night. He brought her to a quiet spot where they could appreciate the beauty of Seattle's night skyline. She often forgot how beautiful her city was. "Thank you for taking me here."

He wrapped an arm around her waist. "No problem."

The scene was very romantic but all she could think about running away, not necessarily to get away from him, but to just be wild. She was feeling restless... crazy. She wanted to be impulsive, irresponsible for once in her life. She was so tired of being the good girl.

She turned to him, a wide smile practically splitting her face in two. "I feel like doing something crazy."

He laughed out loud. "Like what?"

"I don't know..." She worried her bottom lip, trying to come up with options. She couldn't even come up with anything, proof that she was pretty much useless when it came to fun.

"I have an idea or two," he offered. "How about I give you a few options, and you pick one."

She grinned playfully. "Sounds like fun."

11

I SORT OF… DID SOMETHING CRAZY

Cole stared off into the distance, a finger on his bottom lip. She couldn't help but appreciate the man's pure sex appeal. Then why wasn't she climbing all over him? She didn't quite understand it.

"Okay, first off," he started with a wicked smile, "we could get naked and have sex right here."

She laughed. "Oh… of course, you would suggest that."

"Hey, a man's gotta try."

Kirsten had told herself she wouldn't go there yet. Sex only made everything complicated. And she was having so much fun with him. She didn't want to jeopardize that. "Yeah… I'm sure. What else you got?"

He bit his lip again. "You could ride my bike."

She looked at him, wide-eyed. "On the streets of Seattle?"

"No… on farm roads in Northern Canada… of course, Seattle."

She shook her head. No way. This option presented a very real risk of physical injury, not just for her but for him as well. And she would not be responsible for the death of such a beautiful man. "Next…"

"Okay… no bike… How 'bout petty robbery?"

She couldn't believe what he was saying. "What?!"

"We could go into a 7-11, and you could steal something small like a pack of cigarettes or something."

"I don't even smoke," she pointed out. "And don't they keep those behind the counter?"

He cocked a brow. "Okay... that might be a little ambitious," he conceded. "How 'bout a pack of gum or a chocolate bar?"

She didn't like the idea of committing a crime. She wondered if she could end up in a jail cell for something as small as stealing a chocolate bar. She wouldn't do well in a jail cell with a bunch of delinquent women.

She slouched. "I guess I'm just not the wild type."

They stood in silence for a beat or two. "I've never seen you naked," he said out of the blue.

She wondered what he was up to. Back to the sex suggestion, she concluded. Men...

"Do you have any tattoos?" he asked.

She shook her head. She had always thought tattoos could be beautiful. Cole's certainly were. But she had never had the courage to get one. They were so permanent.

"I know a 24 hour place downtown," he told her. "I think they cater to the piss drunk crazy kids."

She laughed. "Like us?"

She thought about it. This was such a crazy night, a crazy time in her life, so many memories; the break-up with Logan, Ethan... Cole. Perhaps something tasteful and small, somewhere discreet on her body, where it could be hidden from the world. It wouldn't be so crazy. When she'd be forty-five with a mini-van, a picket fence and two tweens, it could help her remember that she had been young and crazy once. "I like that option."

His eyes grew wide. "Really?"

She nodded enthusiastically. She had made up her mind.

"They're pretty permanent, you know."

"I know," she said. "That's what makes it so crazy."

TO KIRSTEN'S RELIEF, the place seemed relatively clean and professional. The tattoo artist was a pretty, pink-haired woman around her age. Her arms were covered with beautiful tattoos.

She greeted Cole with a kiss on the cheek. Kirsten concluded that she must have been an old girlfriend. "We got a virgin, here," Cole offered. "I'd like you to meet Kirsten."

She extended her tattooed arm. "Hi... I'm Sandra," she offered. "I'm Cole's sister."

Kirsten smiled. "It's nice to meet you."

Less than an hour later, they were perusing the binders of tattoo designs. For some reason, Ethan had managed to creep up in her mind. He had a tendency to do that. She thought of his wicked smile when he teased her. "Do you have any dragonflies?"

Sandra grabbed the binder from her. "Yep, we do." She fever-ishly flipped through the designs and pointed her purple-tipped finger at three different dragonfly designs. The last one was Kirsten's favorite. It was beautiful and exactly what she had in mind.

"That one." Kirsten pointed. "Somewhere discreet."

"Sure." Sandra smiled. "The first one should always be hidden. See how it feels. How 'bout on the hip?"

Kirsten smiled and she turned to Cole who wore a wicked grin. It was perfect... sweet and a little naughty, just like her.

Kirsten winced as she pushed through the pain, and tried not to look as Sandra worked her magic just above her right hip bone. Cole stood by her for support. "That is going to be one sexy tattoo."

Kirsten laughed, not missing the fact that she was lying next to him, with her dress pulled up and panties pulled down. It was certainly not under the circumstances he would have preferred. "How long does it take to heal?"

"About two weeks," Sandra told her. "We're almost done here. You've been great."

Kirsten winced, yet again. "Trying to be a tough girl."

By the time Cole dropped her off at her place, the sun was rising. She couldn't believe she had pulled an all-nighter. Always the responsible one, she had never done that before. She had also never gotten a tattoo before. Her mother would probably kill her. She smiled as she handed Cole his jacket and helmet back. "Thanks so much," she offered with a sweet kiss on his cheek. "That was... the *best* night."

He grinned. "I'm glad you had fun," he said and then he pulled her to him. "But just so you know... I'm not quite done with you."

And then he released her, and left her standing there as he sped off. Kirsten was motionless for a second or two, trying to work out what he meant. But she was also way too exhausted to even think straight.

She spotted her reflection as she stood by the elevators; disheveled, mascara and eyeliner running. She looked like a rung-out raccoon, her hair in a magnificent almost-artful collection of bird nests. She looked like one of those models in those heroin chic fashion ads. One of her riding boots was all scuffed, and for the life of her, she couldn't remember how that had happened. And to top it off, she had a splitting headache. A tall glass of water, Ibuprofen and a long nap were in order. But the nap couldn't be too long, she reasoned, because her entire schedule would then be messed up.

That's when she saw him exiting the elevator, looking as breathtaking as ever. He did a double-take when he spotted her. Damn, of all the times she could have accidentally run into him, why did it have to be now? As she scurried toward the elevator, he grabbed her wrist. "Wait."

The touch of his hand send a current through her. Why? Why

did it have to be like this? When Cole touched her, it wasn't like this. Why couldn't she feel this energy with him?

He grinned at her. "You look like something the cat dragged in."

She sneered at him. He had barely uttered three words, yet had managed to insult her already. She wasn't in the mood this morning. "Gee... thanks, Ethan."

Her studied her, curious. "Where have you been?"

"Are you keeping track of me?" she asked. "Why do you care?" She didn't quite know why she was being so hostile. She supposed it was a defense mechanism. She was so attracted to him, yet she desperately wanted to get away from him.

He backed up, seemingly hurt. "I'm sorry... you just look..."

She shook her head. "No, I'm sorry," she said. "I've just had a long night, that's all. Cole and I went to a party and then..." She didn't want to elaborate and tell him about the tattoo.

"And then?" he asked, his expression anxious.

She flashed him a smile. She knew exactly where his mind was going, and she decided to let it go there. "Did you know he rides a bike?" she asked. "A vintage Harley. It's almost as cool as your Jag."

He forced a smile. She could see he hated this little tidbit of info. "Well, I'm glad to see he didn't kill you."

"Yep, you can't get rid of me that easily," she quipped as she pressed the button to call the elevator again.

"Yep, I guess not," he said, the words matter-of-fact. Then he turned from her and headed down the lobby.

She watched his tall beautiful frame disappear onto the street, and she sighed a little.

Ethan was so tense. It was a good thing he was heading for an early workout. He'd be able to work the stress away. He really wished he could just get her out of his system. How long had it been since he'd last been with her? A few weeks? He just couldn't seem to shake her. And with

Natasha away in Hawaii, he didn't have anyone else to distract him.

The idea of her sleeping with Cole was driving him insane, which was crazy because he should just be happy for her. This is exactly what he'd wanted for her when they first undertook their little project. But now...

As he made his way to the gym, bag slung over his shoulder, he pictured her on the back of Cole's Harley, clinging to him, and then in Cole's bed, with her legs wrapped around his body.

He wanted to punch something. Luckily, a few jabs on the punching bag would help him work out his anger.

Kirsten crashed onto to her bed, and as she drifted into sleep, she thought only of Ethan.

Two hours later, she woke to the sound of her clock radio. Her head splitting headache had not left her, despite having gulped down Ibuprofen and a glass of water. She also felt the soreness on her right hip. Oh crap, she thought. She had completely forgotten about the tattoo. Her mother would not be impressed. She kind of wanted to rip off the bandage and have a peek, but always the good girl, she behaved.

Her mother was busy typing when Kirsten stepped into her office.

"I got your text," Lorraine told her, not taking her eyes off her laptop screen. "Thanks. Did you have fun?"

"I did," she told her mom. "Is this a good time to talk?"

Lorraine lifted her gaze from the screen. "Yep, I'm just returning some emails."

"I sort of... did something crazy."

Lorraine's eyes grew wide. "What?"

Kirsten winced a little. "I got... I got a tattoo... on my hip."

Lorraine's mouth hung open. "You did not."

Kirsten nodded, biting her bottom lip. "I did."

"Show me."

Kirsten smiled. "It's healing. I'll show you when it looks good."

"That Cole is a rather naughty influence," Lorraine pointed out. "You be careful with him, promise?"

Kirsten nodded in agreement.

"I mean he seems nice enough..."

"He is," Kirsten reassured her mother.

He is nice, she thought again to herself.

Then why isn't he enough?

ETHAN WAS happy Natasha had finally returned from Hawaii. She looked even darker than she had the last time he had seen her. Perhaps tonight would be the night, he thought, the night he would finally forget all about Kirsten.

Natasha studied him as he slaved over a pot of pasta. "Your apartment is amazing," she offered, taking in the space with awe. "It has so much personality."

"Thanks," he replied, busying himself with the salad spinner. He was pulling out all his cooking moves. He wanted this evening to be perfect. It was technically only their second date, but something had to happen, so he could move on and forget all about Miss Beals. "I collect vintage junk."

She laughed. "It doesn't look like junk."

He smiled. "Yes, the price tags definitely would indicate otherwise."

"Expensive?"

"Crazy," he told her. "The hoarder baby boomers are probably making a fortune on eBay."

She shot him another wide smile. She was quite beautiful tonight in a tight blue dress, but for some reason, she still didn't have that pull on him, that mysterious appeal Kirsten did, that invisible 'something' that just made him want to reach out and touch her, run his hands through her hair... kiss her. He shook his head. He didn't understand it.

Natasha helped him set the table. She went all out ; the best linens and dishes, stuff he barely ever used. She also lit up some scented candles and dimmed the lights. It was just a spaghetti and salad dinner with chocolate mousse for dessert, but he appreciated the effort. He smiled and wondered what she really had in mind. Perhaps they were on the same page.

They chatted as they ate. She told him all about her trip to Hawaii; the beach, the amazing private chef they had, the visit to the Pearl Harbour memorial site, the mountains, and the incredible snorkeling. He tried to focus but found himself having a hard time doing so. She didn't ask how the past two weeks had gone for him. If she had, he would have told her 'excruciatingly slow'. But the dinner was pleasant enough and she didn't fail to shoot him a flirtatious smile or two. He knew she was up for more tonight. But strangely enough, he was in no hurry.

Kirsten had been reading her mother's new book all afternoon. She had been completely caught up in it. It was one of her mother's steamier reads. Lorraine wrote under two names. Under her own name, she wrote contemporary family-centered romance. These books were the ones she was so well known for. But she also wrote erotic romance under the pen name Lexie Stone. Kirsten loved these books. They were so passionate and arousing.

But as she feverishly flipped to chapter sixteen, her mind was full of only one person. Not Cole, but Ethan. It was always Ethan.

She shook her head and tried to focus on the story, two kindred spirits who meet on a train, have amazing sex, and fall in love.

HE TRAILS kisses down the inside of my arm.

I reach for his face, desperately wanting to kiss him.

His lips are soft against mine, and his tongue is gentle. He is languid tonight, slow and soft. I want him so much, I'm not sure if I can keep up with his pace.

His mouth travels to my neck and down to my collarbone, trailing kisses. I drown my face in his soft hair, in the wonderful scent of him. I could get buried in that smell.

He slides his hand under the hem of my dress, the palm of his hand sliding against the soft fleshy part of my thigh. I instinctually spread my legs for him, wanting him to touch me.

And he does.

His fingers slip under my lace panties and glide against my lips, wet and slick. He pulls his face away from mine and watches me intently. I don't feel self-conscious under the scrutiny of his gaze. I like him watching me. He studies my expression as the desire builds in me, as I near my climax, my breathing labored, my whimpers louder.

He slides in and out of me. "How do I make you feel?"

"Amazing," I almost groan. He seems pleased. My pleasure brings him happiness. As he digs deeper into me, and his tempo speeds, he brings me closer. I know I am nearing climax. I grip the edge of the seat, not taking my eyes off his. Our gazes are locked.

And then...

He pulls away.

His other hand makes its way under my dress. He leans down and grabs the band of my panties and pulls them down slowly. He kisses the inside of my thigh as he does so. He slides them over my knees, down my legs, and finally over my leopard-print heels.

IT WAS NO USE. The two characters had morphed into her and Ethan. Ethan was the one doing these things to her.

Only he wasn't.

And how she wished he was. He was just next door... he could be. She shook her head. The reality was that she was lying in her flannel pajamas on a Saturday night, reading a book. Yes... this was the real her. She had tried to be someone else, but had miserably failed. She still wanted to be that other person, that fun, free-spirited woman, that daring woman who did crazy things, who made memories she would definitely remember on her death-bed.

She threw the book on the sofa and raced to her room. Thoughts of him were consuming her fully. She had hoped that over the days and weeks, he would fade. But he hadn't. He was always a constant in her mind. She was obsessed. How many weeks had it been since they had made love? Two or three weeks? She cried as she realized that she would never get over him. If a gorgeous sexy man like Cole couldn't help her forget him, then no other man would ever be able to.

She peeled off her flannel pajamas, sat naked on her bed and hugged her knees. She gazed at her reflection in the beautiful antique mirror on the wall of her whimsical room. Her hair was a mess... bed head. And she had no makeup on. She wondered if Ethan would like her like this, natural. She studied the dragonfly on her hip. It had completely healed and it was quite beautiful in its craftsmanship, a real little piece of art right on her flesh. She wondered if Ethan would like it. Obviously she had gotten it with him in mind. She ached to be touched by him, to make love to him again. Once or twice wasn't enough.

Her lips curved into a smile. Tonight was hers. Her mother had gone for the weekend at their cottage for a romantic getaway with Max. And she wondered why she was sitting there on her bed, all alone, in full spinster mode.

Enough was enough.

She bounded to her dresser, a smile on her face, and selected her sexiest underwear, an expensive black laced set with beautiful embroidery and silk ribbon details. She had only worn it once or twice. It hadn't been a good investment so far. She shook her head, fluffing her hair, dabbed on some glossy lipstick, and studied her reflection again. She felt incredibly sexy. And also very aroused.

She grabbed her Burberry trench coat (a must for Seattle), and threw it on. She dashed out of the apartment barefoot. She knew she was acting crazy, but that was exactly the idea.

As she knocked on his door, she prayed he would answer. Her mind was full of all the delicious and naughty things they would do once he opened the door and took her in his arms.

Ethan and Natasha were enjoying the chocolate mousse he had whipped up when he heard a knock at the door. He was surprised. He wasn't expecting anyone. "Excuse me for a second," he told her as he set down his fork. "I'll just be a sec."

When he answered the door, he couldn't believe his eyes. Here was the woman who had consumed his thoughts for the past weeks, standing there, barefoot, in a trench and wearing a curious expression, naughty, terrified, and fun all wrapped into one. God... she was as beautiful as he'd remembered.

"Kirsten..." was all he could manage.

12

...YOU'VE MOVED ON

"Hi," she said, shy.

After a beat or two of stunned silence, he suddenly remembered Natasha sitting in his dining room. He had no clue what was up with Kirsten, but his intuition told him she had something naughty in mind, and every cell in his body wanted to take her in his arms and rip that trench coat off of her.

She worried her bottom lip as she had a tendency to do when she was nervous or ill-at-ease. "I'm sorry to just pop by like this."

"It's uh..." he stammered. "It's okay... it's nice to see you." God... what was he going to do? He couldn't very well tell her he was busy with another woman and turn her away. How he wished Natasha would suddenly disappear into thin air.

Kirsten reached for the belt of her trench with a mischievous glint in her eye. "I wanted to show you something," she started. "I wanted to ask for your opinion," she went on as she started to peel off her trench seductively.

He wanted to stop her but he was frozen. He lost all breath. Why was she so damn beautiful? She looked so vulnerable standing there in front of him wearing nothing but the sexiest underwear he'd ever seen. He wanted to rip it to shreds. And that tattoo... It had to be what she was referring to. He loved it. It was sexy as hell. He wanted to lick it. But all he did was stand there, motionless, in a state of shock.

"Ethan?" Natasha called out as she made her way to the entrance. Ethan turned back, knowing this was the moment he had dreaded. Her jaw dropped to the floor when she spotted Kirsten. Ethan turned back to explain himself to Kirsten, and his heart sank when he saw her expression.

She was shattered. A disturbing mix of emotions played across her beautiful features; hurt, shame, shock. Her eyes welled up as she reached for her trench coat and quickly slipped it back on. "Uh..." she faltered. "I'm... I'm so sorry... I didn't know."

Before Ethan could find his voice, she had dashed out of his apartment. He stood there, still frozen, wanting to run after her. But he couldn't. Natasha was still standing there, shooting daggers at him. "What the hell?" she asked, clearly not impressed.

"I'm sorry, Natasha," he tried to explain. "That's just..." He really didn't know how to explain Kirsten without lying. What was he supposed to say? That she was just a fling he had had, of no consequence. Because he knew that wasn't the truth. She was so much more than that.

Natasha reached for her jacket and purse. "I'm leaving," she told him. "The last thing I need is a player who makes me crappy spaghetti and has little tattooed whores dropping by at all hours."

He almost wanted to smile. The thought of Kirsten as a little tattooed whore made him happy. She was anything but. But she had definitely come a long way. Just the memory of her in that black lace underwear... and that tattoo. He was aroused and he couldn't wait for Natasha to leave. He didn't say anything, didn't try to convince her to stay. He didn't care. All he could think about was Kirsten.

He rapped on Kirsten's door but there was no answer. Then he resorted to screaming. He needed to see her, to touch her, to have her. "Kirsten, please..." he called out as he knocked louder. "I can explain everything."

Finally, the door opened slowly. She was still wearing the trench and her eyes were all puffy and red. He realized he had done this to her. He pushed his way in and grabbed her tightly in his arms, holding her and taking in the wonderful scent of her. He had missed her so much.

She tried to pull away but he wouldn't let go. "I g-guess..." she struggled to say, her voice cracking, "...you've moved on."

"No, I haven't, Kirsten," he tried to make her understand. "I haven't. All I can think about is you. Natasha and I... we haven't..."

She tore herself away from his grasp. "Then why was she at your place? Wearing that dress?"

"I thought she could help me forget," he admitted. "But I was wrong."

"But you were about to sleep with her, right?"

He didn't say a word, not admitting that he would have so quickly jumped to sex with another woman to try to forget her. "And what about you and Cole... I'm sure—"

"Cole and I aren't..." she told him. "All I can think about is you."

He couldn't wait any longer. He had to have her. He pulled her to him by the belt of her trench. And as he struggled to undo the tie, he spotted the pure desire in her eyes. She wanted this as much as he did. He peeled off her jacket and dropped to his knees. He pulled the band of her laced panties with the touch of a finger, and bit at her flesh, at the beautiful dragonfly on her skin. "God... this tattoo is so fucking sexy, Kirsten," he muttered, his breathing ragged. "What were you trying to do to me, dragonfly?"

She flashed him a sly smile. "I just wanted your opinion."

"I love it," he told her as he peeled off her panties. And suddenly, he remembered where they were. "Are we alone?"

She threw her head back and bit her lip, a little move she

always did when she was really aroused. "Yes... my mom is away for the weekend." Her voice was all ragged, broken up. The sound of it made him even harder.

"Lovely," he whispered, his mouth pressed against the soft flesh of her thigh. He didn't know where he wanted to start. He wanted to taste every inch of her, ravish her, feast on her. He had been imagining this exact moment for weeks. And he couldn't hold off anymore.

The feel of Ethan's hot mouth on her thigh was almost more than she could bear. Warmth oozed through her. There was nothing more amazing than this, being with Ethan. She knew she couldn't live without it, and it scared her. She closed her eyes and willed her thoughts away. She would just enjoy him for tonight, and worry about the consequences later. She needed to get her fix. She pulled him up to her, desperately wanting to kiss him. She reached the heavens when his hot mouth pressed against hers. His kiss was hungry. She sucked his bottom lip, wanting to taste him deeper. He buried his hands in the tangles of her hair, his fingers getting caught and pulling at her locks. She inhaled the clean aftershave he wore, wondering for a second if he had put it on for Natasha. It didn't matter. She didn't matter anymore. Because tonight, he was all hers.

"This is all I've been thinking about," he muttered, his hot mouth pressed against the shell of her ear, his hand caught up in the lacy band of her panties.

"Take them off," she pleaded. "I want you."

He pulled his mouth from her and trailed his tongue sensually down the length of her body, sending tingles through her. He was such an amazing lover. She was sure that was the reason she couldn't shake him. "My pleasure."

He peeled the bottoms over her knees and softly down her legs and finally over her bare feet. And he lingered, his mouth dropping feather-light kisses along her thighs. He stroked her softly, the tender touch of his finger sliding along the underside of her knee. He guided her leg over his shoulder and she threw her head as she swelled up for him. She knew what he was planning to do to her, and she had never wanted anything more.

He pressed a finger gently along her soft curls and parted her lips. His hot breath on her pussy sent her to another dimension. There was only him...and her, in this little world of theirs. He licked her softly, and she moaned as he led her closer with every stroke of his tongue. His fingers dug hard into the flesh of her rear as he became more aggressive, responding to her body perfectly. Her climax came in waves of heat, a tingle traveling leisurely up her spine, warming her body along the way.

Her body felt heavy as she leaned against the wall. Ethan was still kneeling at her feet, wearing a wicked smile, and way too much clothing. She felt ill-at-ease, being practically naked, having been pleasured so deliciously. She pulled him up to her. "That was amazing."

He smiled a sweet grin.

She trailed a finger along the soft grey cashmere of his shirt and shot him a sly smile. "As much as I like what you're wearing," she told him. "I'd much rather have you naked in my bed."

A huge grin practically split his face in two as he grabbed her by the rear and hoisted her up on his hips, so easily. "I like that idea." He headed toward the rooms at the back of the loft.

"Last room on the left," she told him. "The door with the flowers."

When they crossed the threshold of her room, if was as if they had entered a fairy tale. Pristine crisp white curtains, an antique gold and white wrought-iron bed dressed in the fluffiest, prettiest comforter known to bedrooms, a myriad of pillows scattered across its top, and Jessie, her cherished teddy bear. It suddenly occurred to her that her room was quite juvenile.

Ethan laughed, a soft chuckle. "Wow," he quipped. "I think I've lost my erection."

She smiled and punched him on the shoulder as he threw her

on the bed, the vintage bed sliding across the hard wood floors and clanking against the wall. "You're going to wake up the neighbor," she joked.

"It's cool. He's not there. He's busy having the most amazing sex of his life."

She smiled. She liked the idea of being 'the most amazing sex of his life'. "So…" she purred. "Let's see about that erection," she said as she pulled him to her, swiftly undoing his belt and fly.

He groaned and bit his lip as she held him and stroked him. "Yep… I don't think the room will be a problem," she teased.

"You are a bad girl."

She made her way down the bottom of his legs and peeled his jeans off. "Yes… there seems to be a misconception about me," she started as she practically ripped his boxers off, "that I'm a good girl."

He laughed. "So obviously not true," he pointed out with a playful smile and leaned down to kiss her. The weight of his body pressed her deep into her cloud of a bed. Her hands busied themselves peeling off his shirt. She wanted the heat of his skin against hers. His mouth trailed along her jawline, biting softly as his fingers struggled under her back to free her from her bra. She reached and helped him.

When her breasts were gently released, he took one in his mouth, twirling his tongue gently. He didn't bite or suck too hard, almost as if he knew she preferred the soft touch. She studied him as his mouth traveled from one breast to the other. Her nipples were red and erect, a reflection of the intense arousal she felt. And even though he had just given her the most amazing orgasm of her life, she craved another one. She yearned for the kind of sex they had had their first time together, fast, hard and furious. She wanted to be pounded nice and good.

She pulled his mouth to hers, wanting to taste it one last time before turning away from him. When she pulled away, she did so reluctantly and turned to her stomach.

"Hey, what's wrong, baby?" he whispered as he sprinkled the length of her spine with soft kisses.

She stretched up, like a Siamese cat, pulling her rear to the ceiling, stretching on all fours, offering all of herself.

"You drive me crazy, dragonfly."

She moaned into the soft cotton of her comforter. He hadn't even entered her yet, but she could almost feel him already. The memory of him combined with the anticipation of what was to come was almost too much to bear. "I want you like this."

He grabbed her hair and pulled it from her nape and licked her one last time before his hands traveled to her rear and grabbed her hard. She guided him as he sank into her. He groaned loudly when his hip bones pressed hard against the soft flesh of her ass.

"Baby..." she breathed. He felt so amazing. There were no words. "Harder, baby."

Which each thrust, he stroked her sweet spot and the old wrought-iron bed clanked against the wall repeatedly, making the lamp on the night table shake, and the framed art on the wall rattle. Her lovely little room seemed like it was about to fall apart any second, but she couldn't have cared less. The dichotomy of the innocence of the room and the raw, uninhibited sex only aroused her.

She shut her eyes. And as the pressure built inside her, she took in every second of the amazing sensations he was giving her as she reached yet another climax. She felt him press into her even deeper, and still as he reached his own, the sound of his pleasure echoing off the walls. Hers had been quiet and soft. She sank deeper into the bed as she recovered. He gently pulled away from her, pressing his mouth against her ear. "Did you... again?"

She nodded, wearing only a tight-lipped smile. "I'm making up for lost time."

He laughed as he lay next to her. "You definitely are. That was amazing."

With her thoughts suddenly clearer, she studied him as he lay next to her, the beautiful angles of his chiseled features, his full sensual lips and the contrasting speckles of dark and light hair spattered along his jawline. He was a work of art. He was the man of her fantasies, but unfortunately, he was also everyone else's. "What happened to your lady friend?" she asked, fueled by feelings of jealousy which refused to escape her.

"She left shortly after your little show," he teased. And Kirsten was glad to see he didn't seem to care. "She called you a little tattooed whore."

Kirsten's mouth hung open. She wasn't sure if she was vexed or flattered. She smiled at the thought. She had certainly never seen herself as a 'little tattooed whore'.

"She didn't mean anything, you know," he told her. "I thought she could help me get over you, that she might make a good girlfriend."

"She was pretty," Kirsten said, pointing out the obvious. "It didn't take you too long to find yourself someone."

His grin was playful when he said, "It's not a big deal... going to a club, buying a girl a drink."

It was so easy for him. It would always be. He was a born charmer. And just the thought of him with other women drove her crazy, made her sick to her stomach. She needed to stop this, whatever this was. She needed to find herself a nice decent man who would not make her feel so irrational. She needed to remind herself that Ethan was not the type of guy who settled down. He would never be. And she still wanted the whole dream; marriage, a home and children. And amazing sex too. That was a given.

Right now, all she had with Ethan was the amazing sex, and it wasn't enough. Her twenty-six birthday was coming up soon and what would she do? Spend the next few years in this limbo, having casual (albeit mind-blowing) sex with Ethan, all the while trying to find someone else and not being able to love anyone because she's too caught up in Ethan? And not to mention, being constantly tortured by feelings of jealousy and anger every time she'd wonder where he was and who he was with. She couldn't live that way.

He was quiet too and she wondered what he was thinking about. He turned to face her and caught her staring at him. There was a hint of tension in his expression. She wondered if she should ask him to leave. She didn't want to get in deeper. "Uh... I was thinking that perhaps... you should go."

The disappointment he felt at her words was unmistakable, and part of her was glad he did feel something, that she hadn't just been another one of his lays. He did seem to really care about her. But was he just playing her?

"Sure..." he said, turning away from her. "If that's what you want."

"You know, Ethan," she started. "It's just for fun between us." She really wanted to believe her own words but even as she uttered them, she knew they sounded false.

He slipped on his boxers and jeans. He searched for his shirt which she found crumpled up in a ball on the bed. She threw it at him. "Isn't this what you like? What you want?" She wanted him to tell her it wasn't. But he didn't say a word. He just fixed her with an angry expression, and left.

She hopped out of her bed, her arms wrapped around her breasts. She ran after him. "I'm sorry," she called out but he was already gone.

Ethan fumed as he paced back and forth across his apartment. He desperately wanted to go back there and tell her off, tell her she couldn't treat him that way, like a piece of meat. She had clearly used him for her own pleasure. She had not only come once, but twice. He'd certainly given her money's worth. And then she had dismissed him so easily. 'Get the fuck out,' she had practically told him. And all she had to do to seduce him was pop by his apartment, wearing nothing but laced undies and a jacket. It had been that easy. He was acting like a cheap whore, and she was treating him like a cheap whore. He had played that role often with other women, but for some reason, it bothered him now. He wanted to be more to her. Maybe she wasn't the girl he thought she was. What had he turned her into? Was she just like everyone else now? Just out for a good time?

He refused to believe that. She was way too sweet, the way she smiled at him, the tenderness of her kisses and her touch. He knew he meant something to her. Then why was she acting like such a bitch?

He couldn't let her treat him this way. And he could clearly not stay away from her. He knew it would happen again. All she had to do was show up at his door and flash him her sweet smile, and he'd be done for. He knew it as surely as he knew the sky was blue, or rather grey, on most days in Seattle. He would have to get away from her.

He needed to make a change.

KIRSTEN WAS EXTREMELY busy at work going over the details for the library fundraiser. She was thankful for the distraction. There were so many details to be taken care of; the menu, the seating, the silent auction, the entertainment. The venue had been selected a long time ago, a large open room at the top of one of the many business buildings in the city cluster. It offered amazing panaromic views of the Seattle skyline, complete with a large deck area to further appreciate the tapestry of colorful lights. The fundraiser had been a grand affair, and every year she looked forward to going. Of course, for the past five years, she had been accompanied by the very charming and successful Logan Smith. His firm was a big supporter.

She dropped by the market after work, as she usually did, to pick up a few staples for dinner. She ran into her mother as she made her way back home. Lorraine was in usual top form, yoga pants (although she had never done yoga in her life), a colorful eccentric top, and a silk lime scarf wrapped around her neck. She took one of the bags from Kirsten. "Here, let me help you."

"Thanks, Mom."

"So what's for dinner?" Lorraine asked as they made their way into the loft building.

"Fish tacos," Kirsten told her. "I just bought some nice mahi-mahi."

A wide smile stretched across Lorraine's face. "You are amazing."

Kirsten was happy she could bring her mother pleasure so easily. It was nice to be appreciated. "Maybe you can help me make a salad," she suggested as she pressed the button to call the elevator. Every time she'd do so, part of her always hoped to see Ethan walk out. And there was always a tinge of disappointment when he didn't, even though she knew the odds were against her. Again, as the doors opened and an older gentleman stepped out, she felt the tinge. How silly, she thought.

Lorraine settled herself in the corner, still clutching the recyclable bag full of goodies. "So I was just having coffee with Deanna Bowen," Lorraine started. "She's a real estate agent, as you know," she went on as they stepped off the elevator. "She had some interesting gossip."

"Oh yeah, what?" Kirsten asked absent-mindedly, turning her key into the door handle.

Lorraine's face lit up when she said, "Guess who's moving out of the building?"

Kirsten jerked her head to face her mother. She knew it was Ethan. She just knew it. "Who?"

"Our handsome neighbor," she whispered, "the ineffable Mr. Fox."

Kirsten's heart sank. She could barely hold on to her bag of staples. She sprinted to the kitchen, her eyes welling up. She didn't want her mother to see her expression. Lorraine had no clue what was going on between her and Ethan. As far as her mother was concerned, Kirsten and Ethan had only shared one or two ill-advised nights, followed by some major drama.

Kirsten busied herself stashing away the staples, and to her dismay, Lorraine insisted on assisting her. "Yep, he just put his loft on the market yesterday. They've already gotten offers but apparently he's asking for a lot. Too much, Deanna says."

Kirsten buried her face in the refrigerator and sucked in a breath of cool air, trying to keep her thoughts at bay, and put up with her mother's banter, despite feeling torn apart, she wanted to hear the details.

"Aren't you glad to be rid of him?" Lorraine asked. "I know you two have had problems and you can't stand the man."

Kirsten nodded, not able to utter a single word, tears threatening to work their way to the surface. How could he do this? How could he just leave like this, without even letting her know? Had what they shared not meant anything? It probably didn't, she couldn't help conclude. Otherwise, he would have spoken to her.

The fish tacos were appreciated by Lorraine but Kirsten could hardly eat a bite. Her appetite had been robbed by heartbreak and anger. She needed to face him. She needed to know why he was doing this. She desperately needed answers. "I'm sorry, Mom, but I've got to go do something for a sec."

Lorraine cocked a brow, curious. "Where? What?"

Kirsten dashed out of the apartment, didn't even bother to put on shoes.

He answered on the second knock. He wore a serious expression and didn't seem completely surprised to see her at his door.

"So you're moving." She jumped right into it. No sense in beating around the bush. "Why didn't you tell me?"

He rubbed his eye with the back of his hand, seemingly irritated. "It all happened really fast. I just decided..."

"Why?"

He fixed her with an intense expression. "Why do you think?"

She didn't quite understand his words. Was he telling her what she thought he was saying, that he was getting away from her? Had she really been so horrible or distracting? Had she brought out the same feelings of confusion and uneasiness in him, as he had in her? "You're trying to get away from me?" she asked, the words soft and trailing with uncertainty.

He shot her a tight-lipped smile. "I need to," he confessed. "You and me... it's too much. And you know I'm not the man for you, and you just want to have fun right now."

"But why move? That seems a little extreme."

He shrugged, hands in pockets. They were still standing at the door. He hadn't invited her in. "I need a change," he told her. "I've been feeling restless. And it'll be exciting to move to a new place."

"But you just moved here," she pointed out. "Less than a year ago."

Kirsten's heart sank deeper. It was over. No more surprise run-ins at the elevators, or naughty pop-ins. He would probably not even leave a forwarding address. He would be completely gone from her life. She couldn't bear it. "Maybe we could keep in touch..." Even as she said the words, she knew this would be a bad idea. A clean break was what they both needed.

He shook his head. "You know you're better off without me, Kirsten."

And with those words, she knew it was over. She knew she would have to accept it and move on. She just didn't know if she could.

13

YOU LOOK WELL-RIDDEN...

Ethan had had just about enough of his real estate agent. She was, yet again, trying to convince him to lower his price. But he refused to do so. He wanted what the place was worth, and he would accept no less.

She clutched a folder of papers in one hand, and a briefcase in the other, looking like she planned to take over the world. "Mr. Fox," she started, shoulders squared. "I've been doing this for a long time. And I can tell you from experience... you will not sell at this price," she pressed, matter-of-fact. "Do you even want to sell?" she asked him, irritation evident in the deep grooves lodged between her brows. "Because honestly, you don't seem very motivated."

She was absolutely right. He wasn't. He wanted to stay.

But he had to do this. There was no way around it. "Drop twenty grand from the price," he conceded. "That's as low as I'm going to go."

She sneered. "Well, that's not going to help much," she told him. "But perhaps if we got rid of these weird vintage pieces you've got everywhere and uncluttered the space, it might show better."

He sighed. Just great. Now to add insult to injury, he also had to put his cherished 'junk' in storage. He was really starting to despise Deanna Bowman.

KIRSTEN RACED in her heels to the little Thai place, clutching a crumbled piece of paper with directions. She hated running late. It implied actual 'running' which she didn't enjoy much, especially in four-inch heeled wedges. She had dressed up a little today because Meghan was always so fashionable and she didn't want to pale in comparison.

She had thought a lot about the lunch with Ethan's sister. It had been planned for a while, postponed and rescheduled. Meghan had a lot on her plate. Kirsten wondered if it was a bad idea. Was she just trying to cling to Ethan by keeping a connection to him through his sister? But Meghan was so nice, and they had gotten along famously. And Kirsten needed a friend.

Kirsten could feel the blush on her face as she took a seat at the small table. The running had increased her heart rate, or perhaps it was just the excitement of seeing Meghan.

"You have to try the mango bubble tea," Meghan cheered. "It's so good."

"Bubble tea," Kirsten said. "I've never had it."

"Really?" Meghan peeked from her menu. "You'll love it."

Kirsten smiled. She loved Meghan's energy. She was very much like her brother. Ethan was like this too, always so 'on', so cheerful. Perhaps that's what she resented about him at first. Introverts like her are sometimes a little threatened by larger-than-life personalities. She and Ethan were so different, she mused. It would have never worked, she told herself as she perused the menu. She decided on a satay chicken appetizer and a green curry shrimp entrée. "You and your brother are very similar," she pointed out. "You look alike. You act similar."

Meghan smiled. "But I have better legs."

Kirsten laughed. "For sure. His are all hairy."

They were both laughing as the server brought their bubble tea. Kirsten was intrigued by the tall milkshakes and the dark pearls resting at the bottoms of the glasses. She ventured a sip through the thick straw. She delighted in the sweet taste and slimy texture as a pearl slid under her palette and down her throat.

"Wow, this is amazing," she cheered. "Why haven't I tried this before?"

"Well, now you have, you crazy girl."

Yes, she had been a little crazy lately, more so than Meghan could ever imagine.

Meghan's face suddenly got uncharacteristically grim. "But speaking of Ethan, he and I... we're not so much alike. He's much more serious than I am. Much more intense."

Kirsten was curious. "How so?"

"Well, he just doesn't take life as lightly as I do. He didn't take it well at all when our mother left us. He hated her."

Kirsten was at a loss for words. "Oh..."

"He told me once that he would never get married," Meghan carried on, "that he would never let a woman hurt him the way our mother hurt our father."

"I guess that's why he's such a player," Kirsten chimed in. "Keeping it casual."

"But he's not really," Meghan argued. "He's always been such a nerd, you know. He used to get teased so much at school. Never had a girlfriend."

"Really?" Kirsten was shocked by Meghan's revelation. For some reason, she couldn't picture a nerdy Ethan Fox. "I can't see it."

"He had these nervous tics when he was younger," she explained. "They were involuntary, throws of the head, grimacing, that sort of thing. He tried medication but it was of no use."

Kirsten abandoned her bubble tea, fully engrossed in Meghan's words. "Now that you mention it... I've noticed him do that little thing with his head here and there."

Meghan smiled. "Yes... most of his tics have faded, but he still occasionally does the head thing," she explained, "but only when he's nervous. You must make him nervous," she added with a playful grin.

Kirsten smiled. The thought of her making the enigmatic Ethan Fox nervous was almost comical.

"He was very lucky to be so intelligent. My father pushed him so hard, seeing his potential. That's all Ethan did. He studied and worked hard, and built his empire," Meghan went on as the waitress served their appetizers, calamari for Meghan. "He never dated. He had no life outside his work."

Kirsten was fascinated. The image she had constructed of this man had been so flawed. They were more alike than she had ever thought. "But he's so slick... such a charmer."

"Well, he's always been a charmer, but people couldn't get past the tics and the nerdy glasses to see the real him."

"Glasses?"

"Yep... he got Lasik surgery and started working out, transformed himself," she carried on between bites of her calamari. Kirsten had barely touched her satay skewers, so engrossed in the conversation. "And all of a sudden, his company went public, and he was rich, gorgeous and Seattle's most eligible bachelor."

"Yep... that's the guy I know."

"Let's just say he's been making up for lost time, these past few years."

Kirsten slouched in her chair, thinking of all the faceless women he'd probably had.

"But I don't think he really ever liked any of them," Meghan mused. "I think he sees them all as superficial gold-diggers, the type of women who wouldn't have given him the time of day

years ago. I think he just uses them to stroke his ego, and probably for the sex too."

Kirsten shrugged "Well, he *is* a man, after all."

Meghan smiled. "Men... can't live with them, can't live without
them."

Kirsten laughed and held up her colorful glass of bubble tea.
"Isn't that the truth?"

As she walked back home, Kirsten thought of Ethan. She realized they were more alike than she'd ever thought. Perhaps that
was the reason he had wanted to help her. He probably saw a
little of himself in her. She understood now that there were deep-
rooted reasons why he would never want to get married. He was
destined to be an eternal bachelor. She felt sorry for him. He
would never experience the true love of a devoted wife, and children who light up at the sight of his face. All because of one
selfish woman's acts. Sure, he was beautiful, rich and successful
with the world at his feet, but his life had already been ruined in
so many ways.

She wanted to reach out and help him, but she knew it wasn't
her place to do so. Their story was over and now he was simply
someone she had known, even possibly loved for a short time.
Her eyes filled with tears at the sadness of it all. All the closeness
they had shared, the words, the smiles, the intimate touches. It
was now all a thing of the past.

ETHAN HAD THROWN himself into his work, not wanting to do
anything else. He still hadn't sold his place and debated whether
to drop the price again. The place was now impeccable; paint
touch-ups, clutter-free, fresh flowers delivered every week. Part of
him was looking forward to moving and starting a new chapter,
and forgetting all about Kirsten. He hadn't been able to do so,
quite yet, but he was sure he'd succeed, in time.

As he scanned his extensive list of emails, he was struck by a particular one, a fundraiser he'd attended for the past few years for the library. His company had been a supporter of the local libraries for years as he believed in its essential services for children who are book and computer-inclined, as he had been as a child. In addition to donations, his company had also been instrumental in the founding of a program which offered free computer science classes, and fostered knowledge in technology for future generations. Yes, this was a dear cause to him, and he would be going again. He realized he'd have to secure himself a date, which wouldn't be a problem. Although, he knew Natasha was now out of the question.

And then in the quickest of flashes, it dawned on him. The library fundraiser. He had never made the connection before. This annual fundraiser... and Kirsten's fundraiser. They were one and the same. He must have brushed past her more than once, he mused. He knew she had also attended these past few years. How in the hell had he never noticed her? He'd have to see her again. He didn't want to miss it, and it would be ridiculous to do so just because of his personal entanglements.

They would both just have to deal with it, and try to act like adults.

ETHAN HAD HAD a rough day at work, and had a splitting headache. He was contemplating whether he had any Ibuprofen left in his medicine cabinet when Lorraine Beals walked up next to him as he stood by the elevators.

"Hello," she said, the word sharp, which was unusual for Lorraine who was always so friendly and charming.

He shot her a tentative smile, not quite knowing where he stood with her. He got the sense it wasn't anywhere good. "Hi, Lorraine. How are you?"

"Well," she replied curtly. "I hear you're moving."

"Yep," he told her. "As soon as I find a buyer."

"I hear you're asking too much," she remarked as they entered the elevator.

"I just don't want to be ripped off, that's all."

"Well, it's for the best," Lorraine added as she pressed the button to their floor. "Kirsten will be much better off with you gone."

His breath hitched at the sound of Kirsten's name. "Uh... what do you mean?"

She didn't utter another word as she stared daggers at him. The silence in the elevator was disquieting. He wanted to crawl out of his skin. When he heard the ding, he let out a breath of relief.

"You've hurt her very much, you know," she told him as they stepped off the elevator, "using her the way you did."

What was this woman talking about, he couldn't help but wonder. "What are you—"

She stopped dead in her tracks and jerked her head toward him. "You might have just been having a little fun. But for Kirsten, it meant much more. She's not the kind of woman who has casual flings. If she was with you, it's because she was crazy about you."

Ethan was speechless. They both stood in the middle of the hall, staring at each other. She was right. He had been kind of a jerk. But so had Kirsten.

Lorraine carried on with a flip of her bouncy curls. "She's trying to move on with Cole, but I know he doesn't rock her boat like you do. And Lord knows why," she added with a scowl. "He's better looking than you, nicer than you, and he rides a motor-cycle for heaven's sake."

Her words got to him. He hated the thought of Kirsten moving on with Cole. "How do you know he doesn't rock her boat?" he asked, knowing very well Lorraine Beals was an over-sharer.

She tilted her head and hesitated, but only for a second. "She hasn't slept with him yet, hasn't really done much except for one kiss," she went on. "She told me all about it yesterday over tea." She fixed the floor when she added, "Kirsten's only been with two men... including you, so yes, Ethan, I imagine you meant the world to her." He could see the emotion in her eyes when she added, "And you... you just disposed of her and shattered her heart to bits."

She walked away but he quickly caught up with her, grabbing her by the wrist. "You're wrong," was all he said. Unfortunately, he didn't know how to express everything he had to say, that Kirsten meant the world to him too, that she was the most amazing woman he'd ever met, and the only one he'd ever loved. Loved... yes, he *loved her*. He *loved* Kirsten Beals. He realized all this, a revelation which had been buried inside him. Until this moment.

Lorraine's voice softened. "This move is a good thing," she said with kinder eyes. "I could see how hurt she was when I told her you were moving. She didn't think I could tell, but I know her too well. But you're doing her the biggest favor in the world, Ethan," she told him as she turned her door handle. "Maybe now, she can finally get over you," she added before disappearing.

What was he doing? What was he waiting for? He needed to tell Kirsten how he felt. Even if she didn't feel the same way, there was nothing to lose. He paced the floors of his loft as he tried to devise a strategy. There was the fundraiser coming up... He had to take action soon because she was the one for him. He had finally found her, the woman who was worthy of his love, the one who wouldn't hurt him the way his mother had. He was tired of the bachelor life. He hadn't enjoyed it much for over a year now. In fact, he had never truly enjoyed it. He realized that deep inside, he had always hoped to find someone special amongst all the beautiful shallow women. And now, it had finally happened, just not in the way he had imagined it. It had caught him by surprise. Kirsten wasn't anything like the woman he had imagined.

She was even better.

KIRSTEN CLIPPED ON A BEJEWELED BROOCH, the final touch to her hair. She wore it in an elegant up-do with curly tendrils framing her face. The look was both elegant and sweet, which was how Kirsten saw herself. The dress she had chosen for the occasion was a classic black gown with a sexy open back. It swished and skirted the floor as she walked in her tall elegant heels. She felt like a modern-day princess.

She wondered what Cole would wear. She prayed to the gods that he didn't show up in black jeans and a white t-shirt. He didn't seem like the dressing-up type. She thought about Logan, for the first time in a long time. He would most undoubtedly show up looking dashing, like he had the past few years. But this time, he would have someone different on his arm, the very beautiful, very flexible Lisa. And then she thought about Ethan. She wasn't sure why. He wouldn't be there. But just the occasional thought of him in one of his slick designer suits got her blood flowing.

She shook her head. Ugh. When would she get the man out of her head? Ever?

She kissed her mother good-bye.

"You look amazing," Lorraine offered. "I've created such a beautiful human being."

Kirsten smiled. Yes, it was always about Lorraine. "Bye Mom... I love you."

Lorraine shot her a wink as Kirsten reached the door. "Be good now."

"Oh... I will," she told her mother, wondering if she really would. Perhaps it was time to move on. Maybe tonight would be the night she would finally give Cole what he clearly wanted.

As she spotted him on his bike in the distance, she hurried, her heels not quite keeping up with her. He was gorgeous in a beautiful tux, clutching two helmets. *Yes,* she thought. *He seems like the type who could show a girl a good time in bed. I could do a lot worse.*

As they flew through the busy streets of Seattle, her arms wrapped around Cole, Kirsten felt young and invincible. She was living life, just as she had vowed to do. She was being wild and crazy. Cole had brought her out of her shell. With him, she could be uninhibited because she didn't care. But with Ethan, there had always been a certain energy between them, something that scared her, that made her feel vulnerable, that kept her cautious. This was what she loved about Cole. It was so easy.

Kirsten was a little disheveled when she got off the back. She hadn't really thought this through, a ride on a bike in an evening gown is not exactly well-advised. She knew she would need to touch-up her hair.

Cole winked at her as she took off her helmet. "You look well-ridden," he teased.

She couldn't help but smile. He was such a tease. "Oh... I think I was," she told him. "But perhaps a little more riding later," she added with a playful smile.

Yes... this evening was definitely starting on the right note.

When Kirsten entered the banquet space, she was awestruck. It was all so beautiful. The theme was 'starry night', very refined and tasteful, the opposite of most high school proms. Twinkle lights and tulle accents caught the eye but didn't quite jump out at you like a jack-in-the-box. The impeccable tables were dressed in crisp white linens and accented with gorgeous candle center-pieces. They were scattered across the room like clouds in a dark sky. It was all so magical.

Kirsten held on to Cole's hand as she entered the space and

offered a few smiles to people she recognized, mostly volunteers, the very young and the retired, it seemed. Many people devoted their time to the cause every year. Kirsten felt a little guilty because she was being paid for her work. Although, tonight, she was off the clock and wasn't being paid, yet she knew she'd still have a lot to look after. She made a mental note to speak to Kendra, the decorator, and praise her for a job well-done.

"Pretty swanky," Cole observed. "This is fantastic."

Kirsten smiled. "I'm so happy. This is the most beautiful I've ever seen it."

She was happy but also nervous, as she always was at this yearly event. After all, it was an accumulation of weeks of work. Everything absolutely had to go smoothly. "As you can see, we're a bit early. I had to come in early to check in on everything."

"No problem," Cole told her. "I'll just hang out while you do what you do."

She stretched her body and kissed him on the cheek. "You are wonderful."

She scurried across the space, the flowy skirt of her evening dress swishing. She checked on the silent auction, the seating chart, the food preparations, and even talked to the band who were busy setting up. Four handsome young men who called themselves 'Kingston Road'. They had all grown up on the same street. They were dressed in suits for the occasion but she knew them as grungy guys who did folk-pop covers of popular songs. The lead singer had an angelic voice and his name just happened to be Ethan too.

Ethan. She hadn't quite been able to not think about him, even on such a busy day. This drove her crazy. The man was gone from her life. Why couldn't she just accept it and move on? Her brain told her to do so, but her heart was being quite pig-headed.

She practically danced around the room, adding final touches, making sure everything was perfect. With the use of a very handy trolley, she made a trip to the storage room and stowed away a few unsightly extras such as crates, boxes, and extra lights, mostly stuff they would only need when the night was over. As she found herself alone in the small dark room, she leaned against an industrial shelving unit, closed her eyes and let out a long breath. She took a moment to regain her composure before the big event, before the guests arrived, before she would have to face Logan for the first time since the break-up.

She was glad to have Cole by her side, glad that she wouldn't have to face Logan alone. She thought of Cole and his beautiful eyes and sexy smile and she imagined him with her in this dark little storage room. A playful smile stretched across her lips as she imagined herself wrapped around him. But suddenly, his steely grey-blue eyes took on a more tropical sky shade, and his dark hair turned golden, and his smile stretched wider, his cheeks fuller, and there they were... those adorable dimples. Damn it, she cursed herself.

Damn you, Ethan Fox. Get out of my head.

14

...SHE'S CRAZY ABOUT YOU

As the first guests made their way in, Kirsten's heart pounded against her rib cage. But as she got to chatting with various people she knew from previous years, she started to relax a little. She promised herself she would have fun tonight, and forget all about Logan. And Ethan too.

She enjoyed a bit of food as trays of appetizers made their way across the room. The band was in full-swing, a soft folk rendition of Madonna's *Crazy for You* filling the room.

That's when she saw him. He was as dashing as ever, wearing an expensive suit, an air of superiority, and a brunette on his arm. The woman was pretty but not the one she had expected. What had happened to Lisa, the yoga instructor? She studied Logan for the longest time, seeing him in a whole different light, how she might see him if he were a total stranger. Yes, he was handsome in a preppy buttoned-up way. And he seemed so self-assured in his tailored suit and expensive loafers. But she knew that behind the façade, there was a self-conscious scared little boy, always kissing people's asses. He was speaking to an older gentleman when he spotted her and did a double-take. Suddenly, he seemed to lose all interest in his conversation and quickly begged off.

He flashed her a bright smile as he made his way to her. "You look amazing."

"Thank you," she replied with a tight smile.

"You've done a wonderful job," he offered. "It seems you outdo yourself every year."

She tilted her head to the side. "Thanks."

He winced. "Listen, I know I'm probably not the person you want to see at the moment, but..." he went on, quickly scanning the crowd. "You're the one I want to see. I've been looking forward to seeing you again."

She sucked in a deep breath. Why was he playing her like this? "Where's your tattooed yoga instructor?"

He smiled a tight grin. "She and I are done."

Kirsten couldn't help be pleased by this. Karma had done its work. "She got bored with you, just as I predicted, I'm sure."

He cocked a brow. "You were right. She and I were not meant for each other. Not like you and..." he trailed off, and she was glad he did because the last thing she wanted from him was a big love revelation.

"So who's your date?" she asked as she caught the pretty brunette's eye. She seemed to be tangled up in a conversation with the older gentleman Logan had been speaking to. Kirsten wanted to rescue her.

"Oh... that's Sandy," he told her, "a paralegal from work... she and I are friends," he carried on, trying to explain. "I just needed a date."

Kirsten shook her head. "I'm sorry. I was just being polite. I really don't care." Sure, she was being blunt, but that's all he deserved. Cole made his way to them with two glasses of white. He handed one to Kirsten as she introduced him. "This is Cole Winters," she said matter-of-factly.

Logan stretched out his hand. "Logan Smith." His expression was business-like and reserved. It reminded her of a hockey game she had gone to a few years back, of the expression the losers had on their faces when they skated across the length of the ice. They shook their adversaries' hands with expressions of defeat, pure defeat.

Kirsten took delight in this, in the sight of the two men next to each other, one clearly superior to the other in terms of size and looks... and presence. She tangled her arm in the crook of Cole's. "It was nice to see you again, Logan."

Of course, Cole had no clue who this man was. Kirsten had never mentioned him by name. "Let's go check out the auction," he suggested and she nodded, wanting to make a quick escape.

As Kirsten perused the details of a spa get-away, she debated whether it would be something worthwhile for her and her mother. When she concluded that yes, it could be fun, she wrote an amount at the bottom of the list, hoping she would be the last to bid. But right next to her, stood a tall blonde, clearly interested. Damn, she thought, she would need to come back and up her bid. When she looked up to offer her a friendly smile, she was taken aback.

"Hey, Meghan," she squealed like a junior high girl. "What are you doing here?"

Meghan smiled, her perfect teeth gleaming as always. "I..." she started, turning her head.

And that's when Kirsten saw him. God... he was stunning, just standing there, wearing a dark tailored suit and a shy smile. He inched closer, hesitating, his smile slowly fading.

"Hi, Kirsten," he offered. "I bet you're surprised to see me here."

She was. She was speechless.

He carried on. "You know, I've come to this for four years now," he explained. "The library is one of the organizations I'm involved in. I can't believe I never told you. All this time, we must have brushed past each other, not knowing..." The expression in his eyes was full of whimsy, of awe. She wasn't sure what he was saying. Not knowing... what? But it was true. It was pretty unbelievable that she would never have noticed him before. She really must have been caught up in Logan and her work. She finally found her words. "It is pretty crazy."

They stood for a beat or two, staring at each other. His eyes were just as consuming as ever. And suddenly, she had the urge to grab him and drag him to the back and lock both of them up in the storage room... forever.

"I never made the connection before," he went on. "You, the library... the fundraiser. I think I was a little distracted..." he added with a playful smile.

She smiled, remembering their early days. "Yes... you were distracted with your devious plans of turning me into Seattle's most tempting seductress."

He laughed. "Well, I believe I did an okay job in that department."

She smiled, shy. As much as she wanted it to be over with him, she was overjoyed to be standing there, talking to him. In fact, she wanted to stand there for eternity.

Ethan couldn't believe how beautiful she was, in her elegant long black dress and her hair in an up-do, curls framing her delicate face. She looked like a beautiful classic actress, a perfect black and white vintage photo. He wanted to take her picture, frame it and hang it on his wall. And she hadn't greeted him with any animosity which he was thankful for. He really hadn't known what to expect. He knew she would be surprised to see him there.

He wondered if she came here alone, and wondered if she and Cole were still an item. And then he saw him walking up to her, looking good, all cleaned up. He felt a heaviness at the pit of his stomach. The feeling was foreign. No other woman had ever brought that out in him; physical discomfort. Man, he had it bad, he realized, a little too late. He loved her. He loved her, and there she was, on the arm of another man. And not just any man, a gorgeous tall man, who looked like that vampire from that silly show his sister loved.

Damn, how he had messed everything up, he mused as he sat next to Meghan. If only he had treated Kirsten with the kindness she deserved right from the start. Karma was coming around to kick him in the ass, and he deserved it. It was probably too late for them now, he thought as he drained his sorrows in a glass of red.

"Jeez, Ethan," she said. "You look like that time on Christmas morning, when Dad forgot to play Santa."

He remembered that morning. Much too clearly. It was the first Christmas without his mother. And his father had forgotten about 'Santa'. And that was the year he also realized there was no Santa. "That's exactly how I feel."

She sighed heavily. "Ethan..." she said softly. "Just go to her. Tell her how you feel."

He jerked his head up. He hadn't realized how transparent he was.

"I know you better than anyone else," Meghan told him. "And I can tell that you've got it pretty bad for her."

He couldn't deny it. He remained speechless, sulking, tracing the tip of his finger along the stem of his wine glass.

"And you know what I can also tell," she went on, "just from the look on her face when she saw you tonight... she's crazy about you too." She tilted her head to the crowd, her gaze fixing the distance where Kirsten sat next to Cole as the server presented them with their appetizers. "I know she has a boyfriend... and it's quite new, I think," she admitted. "But I've had lunch with her, hung out with her. And she talked more about you than she did about her boyfriend. In fact, she barely mentioned him at all. I know when I was first dating Kyle, he was all I could talk about. And funny enough, you're all she could talk about when we had lunch."

Ethan contemplated his sister's words. Perhaps she was right. Maybe it wasn't too late. He had to give it a shot.

15

MAY I CUT IN, SIR?

Dinner had been stellar, but Ethan hadn't been able to appreciate it, his mind too full of Kirsten. He couldn't help but watch her in the distance. Even as the nice couple next to him entangled him in conversation, his gaze still couldn't be pulled away from the delicate beauty at the other side of the room. He had caught her looking at him too, but she always jerked her gaze away, like a naughty little school girl up to something bad, and he liked that. In fact, he loved that. It aroused him. He sighed. There he was at a very formal dinner, sitting amongst strangers, in a state of semi-arousal.

He wanted the minutes to speed along, so he could go talk to her, profess his love. But how was he supposed to do that exactly, he wondered. Pull her from her conversations in the middle of dinner? No, he'd have to wait. And he'd have to be brave. Suddenly, he felt like his old self again, self-conscious, afraid of rejection. But he knew he had to do it, or he would never forgive himself for not trying, for letting the woman of his dreams slip from his grip, into another man's arms.

The band was in full swing performing a rendition of Ray Charles' *What'd I Say*, and everyone was enjoying their strawberry shortcake with a side of chocolate sauce. Kirsten usually loved dessert but her stomach was all caught up in knots. Ethan's eyes were fixed on her, far in the distance. The effect he had on her was amazing, the way he made her feel with just a look. She didn't have that with Cole. She would never have that with him. She never even had that with Logan. Chemistry is a funny thing, she mused. Why one man and not the other?

All she knew was that she was sitting next to one man, and desperately craving another. It wasn't fair to Cole. He seemed to genuinely like her, and she was leading him on. She hadn't meant to, of course. And finally taking the next step and giving him what he wanted was not the answer. If she was going to have sex with a man, she wanted it to be because her body and heart craved it, longed for that man's touch. There was really no other reason to share one's body with another, as far as she was concerned.

As she watched Cole in conversation with a redhead sitting next to him, she realized what had to be done. She couldn't keep leading him on like this. He was a gorgeous man, and undoubtedly had troves of women waiting for him to be on the market again. Or perhaps he already was. They hadn't exactly been exclusive. Either way, she had to set him free.

She led him to the balcony. The night was warm and beautiful. It would have been romantic in other circumstances. Cole eyed her with a cocked brow.

"That redhead seems to like you," Kirsten ventured with a playful smile. "Funny enough, her date doesn't seem to mind."

He laughed, fine lines etching the corners of his eyes. "That's her brother," he told her. "There's actually a funny story there. Her brother just got dumped earlier today. That's why Jessica had to fill in."

Kirsten smiled. "Jessica..."

He took her hand. "I'm here with you."

"Do you like her? She's quite pretty."

A touch of irritation skirted across his features. "I told you. I'm here with you."

She smiled, not wanting to explain, but she had to. "It's not that... I'm not jealous," she started. "It's just that you and me... it's not..."

He winced a little. "I was afraid of this, of this conversation. You're right. You and me..."

She bit her lip. "I don't know what's wrong with me. You're gorgeous. You're amazing."

He laughed. "Yeah, this is new to me. Usually I have a woman in bed by now."

She smiled. "I know I'm crazy."

He inched closer and took both her hands in his. "You're not crazy," he told her, his words soft. "You're in love. Unfortunately, it's just not with me."

She was speechless at his words. How did he know?

"It's pretty obvious," he told her. "The way you two look at each other... the way you interact. I even noticed it on our first date."

"I'm sorry," she offered, sheepish. She felt like such a little misleading tease.

"It's okay," he told her. "I thought I was imagining it but then... I saw you two together again tonight."

"I don't know what to do," she confessed. "He's all I can think about but I don't have the courage to..."

"You need to tell him how you feel," he said. "You owe it to yourself... and to him."

"You think?"

"Definitely." He smiled wide. "But first, you owe me a dance. One last dance."

She grinned at him playfully. "You've got it."

Kirsten had disappeared. Both she and Cole were nowhere in sight. How was he supposed to profess his love to her if she wasn't even there? Perhaps they had gone early for the night, to ravish each other in his bed. He couldn't help but imagine the scene, her ripping off his suit in a frenzy, their limbs tangled in the sheets of his unmade bed, in the middle of his messy artist loft.

Ethan's chest tightened at the thought. He really had to stop doing this to himself. He was digging himself into an early grave. But he couldn't keep the disturbing thoughts at bay. Next came visions of the two of them making out in the coat check room. He rubbed his face frantically, trying to erase the unwelcome images.

Then he saw them, heading toward the dance floor, hand in hand, all smiles. Damn, they seemed so happy. He was pretty sure he didn't stand a chance. He started to have second thoughts. Perhaps he was being selfish, trying to break up a clearly happy couple. Perhaps he should just walk back home with his tail between his legs. But he couldn't do that. He just couldn't. He had to tell her how he felt. She needed all the facts before she decided who she wanted to be with.

As he watched them dance, the jealousy gathered into a thick ball of pressure at the pit of his stomach. He couldn't stand watching them. She looked so beautiful in the tall man's arms. But Cole seemed too tall for her. Ethan approximated his height at about six foot two, roughly about two inches taller than himself. Yes... too tall, he concluded. She'd be better off with him.

But how was he supposed to tear her away from this Greek god? He'd have to use all the arsenal at his disposal, which consisted mostly of the physical connection they had. Because if there was one thing he was sure of was their chemistry. Every time they looked at each other, touched... the world seemed to light up. He'd have to play with that, use that to seduce her. Because he knew he could do that. He'd done it before, more than once. She'd melted under his stare, under his touch. The memories of that made his breath hitch.

He had to go to her.

As he walked up to the couple on the dance floor, his heart

raced a hundred miles a minute. All his senses were heightened. The band was too loud, and the lights were too bright.

His feet dragged as he closed in on them. And finally, he stopped right next to Cole and caught her eye, and he didn't miss her expression of surprise. "May I cut in, Sir?"

Cole smiled warmly at him. "Sure," he said as he retreated. Ethan was surprised by the man's reaction, and relieved as well. He had half-expected a rebuttal and he hadn't wanted a confrontation. He wasn't sure who would come out on top if it came to blows.

He pressed his hand gently on Kirsten's small waist. She didn't say a word and looked at him with was seemed like desire, but he wasn't quite sure. He'd have to test her. She was so beautiful. She made everything around her amazing. Suddenly, the twinkling lights were perfect, the song just right. He wanted to dance with her all night.

As he took her hand in his, he played his plan over in his mind. How would he proceed? He would seduce her slowly to start and study her reaction. And if he sensed the slightest reservation, he would back off. But if she melted into him again...

Then all bets would be off.

Kirsten couldn't believe the turn of events. It felt so right, so perfect being in Ethan's arms. He was being quite the gentleman, and she wanted him to be anything but. Her heart pounded as they danced and she wondered if he could tell. But he wasn't close enough. She was sure he couldn't. She wondered if his heart was beating as fast as hers.

With every twirl of the room, he inched closer. And his breath on her shoulder became hotter, spreading warmth through her. His hand lingered on the side of her waist and then... just as she had hoped, it traveled leisurely to her rear. With barely a touch, he was arousing her already. She wanted more. She trailed her hand from his shoulder to the nape of his neck, wanting to touch his skin, wanting him closer. Suddenly, there were just the two of them in the room.

"You're beautiful tonight," he whispered against the shell of her ear. "I've been watching you all night."

"I've noticed," she said, her breath jagged. How could she have become so turned on from just a dance? "I've been watching you too."

"Uh-huh," he said, his voice soft and delicious. "You wicked girl."

He was driving her crazy. "You've taught me well."

"Yes, it appears I'm an excellent teacher."

Damn, she wanted him. Right then. She craved the taste of his tongue, the feel of his soft stomach, the sensation of him hard for her. "Let's... go..." she faltered, her words all over the place, "...out of here."

He took her hand and led her toward the balcony. She had somewhere a little more private in mind, like that dark storage room, but anywhere with him would do.

As they stepped out, Kirsten took in beautiful Seattle. The flickering colorful lights were dancing and the night was magical. They rushed past the few people scattered across the balcony. They retreated to a little dark corner, secluded from everyone.

"God... I've missed you," he whispered as he pressed his lips against hers. It was everything she had wished for, his warmth pressed against her body, the sweet taste of his mouth. She wanted more. She wanted him naked, deep inside her. As he caught her bottom lip between his, she wondered if it would always be like this between them, high drama, intense sex... the need, the craving. Was this all there was to them? Was this all she was to him? Amazing sex?

She pulled reluctantly from him. "Ethan... we can't," she whispered. "Not here."

"I know," he conceded with a pained expression. "I just want you so badly."

Her gaze fell to the stone floor. "Is this all you want from me?" She couldn't look at him because she was too afraid of his answer. She didn't even want to ask the question. But she had to.

He pressed his fingers against her chin and tilted her head to face him. "Look at me, dragonfly," he said, his voice stern. "Look at me when I tell you I love you."

Her breath hitched. He loved her.

"This isn't just about sex," he went on, dead-serious. "For the first time in my life, this isn't just about sex for me. I love you, Kirsten. I've never loved anyone before. I've been searching for you all my life... for someone to prove to me that there is true love, to believe in someone I can love, someone who won't hurt me." His expression softened as he added, "And I've finally found her."

Kirsten eyes welled up, her heart brimming with emotion. "I love you too, Ethan. You're all I can think about. No other man has ever made me feel the way you do. It's only you."

He smiled, a sweet grin. "You and Cole..."

"We just broke up," she told him. "I just broke it off when I realized I was completely leading him on. You were all I could think about."

He pressed his lips against hers again. She reveled in his kiss but as she felt herself being lifted, caught up in him again, she pulled away. "Hey baby, we probably shouldn't start something we can't stop."

His grin was wicked when he whispered. "Although the night is still young, I think you need to go home and get to bed, young lady."

She smiled wide. "Oh yes, I agree wholeheartedly. Let's go."

Kirsten was filled with anticipation as they gathered her clutch and shawl from the table and raced past the dance floor on their way out. She couldn't wait to have him naked and all over her. Tonight they would make love until sunrise, not miss an inch of skin.

She nipped at Ethan's heels, and struggled to keep up with his long strides.

"Kirsten," she heard her name called out in the distance. Both she and Ethan turned around to see Logan closing in on them.

"Are you on your way out?" Logan asked, curious.

Her heart was pounding like a jack hammer. From the racing around? From being surprised by Logan? From the impending sex? She wasn't sure. "Oh, Logan," she said, completely breathless. "Yes... I was just leaving."

Logan lifted his head as he took in the enigmatic Ethan Fox, and Kirsten delighted in his expression, quizzical awe. Who was this vision of a man? She had always known Logan to be a curious man, and she knew he was just dying to know who this man was.

"That's too bad. We didn't even get to dance," he pointed out with a sly grin, "for old times' sake."

Kirsten smiled. He didn't even instigate anger in her anymore, because she simply didn't care. He had morphed into a caricature.

"Yep... that's too bad," she added as she set out to leave.

Logan extended his hand to Ethan. "Logan Smith."

Ethan offered him his dashing smile. "Ethan Fox."

"Oh... Ethan Fox," he said, wide-eyed. "I've heard of you," Logan told him, as if this little tidbit would suddenly make them best friends. "Funny," Logan added. "You're the second one I've met tonight. Where did your other date go to, Kirsten?" he added playfully, and Kirsten knew he was trying to stir the pot. She knew him too well.

"That was Cole," Ethan chimed in. "He's a friend of Kirsten's," he added with a smile. "But me... I'm the one, the one she's going to marry one day."

Kirsten's heart skipped a beat. And Logan seemed taken aback too. She didn't quite know who was more surprised by this revelation. She stood speechless as Ethan carried on.

"I actually wanted to thank you, Sir," Ethan told him. "If you hadn't been foolish enough to let her go, she and I would have never gotten to know each other and never have fallen in love. So I owe you all the gratitude in the world."

Logan stood, jaw hanging, speechless.

"Now, if you'll excuse us," Ethan went on, towering over Logan. "We're trying to hurry back to my place. I'm planning to make sweet love to my beautiful girlfriend. And then I'll do it all over again, but the second time, I plan to make her scream," he added with a wicked smirk. "And I can't very well do that if we keep chatting with her annoying pretentious ex, now can I?"

Logan stood speechless. In fact he hadn't uttered a single word for quite a while now. Kirsten tried to bite down a smile but couldn't quite do it. She exploded into laughter as Ethan winked at her and grabbed her hand. They raced out of the crowd, both wearing Cheshire cat grins.

Suddenly, she didn't want to wait for the ride home. She wanted him right then. As they raced past the storage room, she pulled him back. "Wait, I've got the perfect little spot for us."

And as they stepped into the small dark space, he pressed her against the storage shelf and whispered against her ear, "I love you, you wicked little dragonfly."

As they made their way to Elliot Bay, Kirsten sulked a little. She had no reason to. It was a beautiful night in Seattle, and she was madly in love. As she and Ethan walked hand in hand through the troves of tourists, he smiled at her. "You need to do it," he teased. "Just jump in."

She glared at him. "I told myself I'd never go on that thing again."

As they made their way to the ticket booth, Ethan laughed. "You need to face it. You see it every day. Hell, we have the best view of the Wheel in our own living room."

She smiled. "Yeah, I'm glad you never sold your place."

He pulled her closer to him as they stood in the line of eager tourists. "It's time to replace the old miserable memories with new happy ones," he added with a kiss on her cheek. "We'll have fun. I promise."

As they stepped into the VIP Gondola car, she couldn't help but squeal a little. "This is so much better than last time," she told him as she settled her rear on one of the luxurious red leather seats. "This rocks."

He flashed her his amazing smile as he took a seat next to her. "I'm glad you're happy."

"Why wouldn't I be," she said, her eyes on the ground below her feet. "Better seat, better company... and check out this glass floor... it's so crazy."

She gazed up and caught him looking at her, the way he always did, with adoration and love. Logan had never looked at her that way. Not even once. She thought back to her last time on the Great Wheel. As she had been going up in the sky, she had not been thinking about how much she loved Logan and how much she wanted to spend the rest of her life with him. She had been thinking about the wedding day, the dress, the flowers, the brides-maids. She had never truly loved Logan. Not in the way she loved Ethan. She pulled her eyes from the Seattle skyline to look at her beautiful man. Not only was he beautiful outside, but inside as well.

As they slowly made their way up, they took in Elliot Bay and the beautiful Seattle skyline at night. The twinkling lights were magical. She glanced occasionally at Ethan. His smile was sweet. But he seemed nervous and not quite himself. She cocked a brow as she studied him.

When they finally reached the highest peak and their gondola swayed at the top, he did a quick a jerk of his head as he reached into his pocket. She smiled because he seemed nervous. That adorable tic was a tell-tale sign. What was he up to?

When he pulled out a pretty blue velvet box, she knew. Tears of happiness made their way to the surface at rocket speed and her words caught in her throat. She was speechless. It was all too much. Ethan wore a sweet expression as he opened the velvet box and presented her with the most beautiful diamond ring she'd ever seen; white gold, dragonfly design, a gorgeous diamond flanked by a myriad of smaller ones.

She wanted to say 'yes' but had suddenly lost the ability to vocalize.

His smile faded slowly as he watched her, sudden concern clouding his features. Oh no, she thought. Thankfully, she found her words again. "Yes... yes, I'll marry you, Ethan."

A huge grin practically split his face in two as he took her in his arms. "I love you, Kirsten."

"I love you too, Ethan."

He held on to her tightly, and she didn't want him to ever let go. "How's that for a new memory?" he asked.

She laughed, her eyes full of happy tears. "Amazing... the best."

The end.

ACKNOWLEDGEMENTS

I would like to thank my amazing husband and kiddoes.
I would also like to thank all my amazing readers, and all the
wonderful readers on Wattpad who originally made this story a
success. It received 2.3 million reads!!! And also tons of comments
and wonderful feedback. And many thanks to all those who have
shared my books, whether it be by telling a friend, writing a
review, or sharing on social media. Thank you to all the
wonderful bloggers who have supported *The Ground Rules
Trilogy*, *The Riverstone Series*, the **One Week** series, and the
Orchard Heights series. You have no idea how much that means.
Reviews are crucial and word of mouth is key. Without all of you,
I wouldn't be here.
Again, thank you to my wonderful Beta readers, Chancy, Geneva,
Melissa, Veronika, and Louise. You gals are all amazing, and good
friends. I can't thank you all enough. I'm very lucky to have
you all.
And finally, thank you to all my book friends!

ABOUT THE AUTHOR

Roya Carmen is a book junkie, self-professed chocoholic and hopeless romantic. A graduate of Ryerson University, she worked in Graphic Communications before becoming a stay-at-home mom. She has always loved writing, finding her passion for romance in 2008. She enjoys spending time with her family, camping, playing billiards, and painting. And of course, there is nothing she enjoys more than sitting down at her laptop and making up stories – and if those stories should include beautiful men, a little romance, and a few steamy scenes, all the better! Roya lives north of Toronto with her husband and three children.

ALSO BY ROYA CARMEN

To check out all my books, please check my Amazon profile at:
https://amzn.to/2MTAY5l

The Ground Rules Trilogy - International bestselling erotic romance trilogy.

The Riverstone Series – A series of steamy standalone reads.

One Week Series - A series of steamy standalone reads.

Orchard Heights series - A series of steamy standalone reads.

Back to You (The You Collection) - A sweet summer romance.

Only You (The You Collection) - A steamy summer novella.

Read below for more detailed info.

The Riverstone Series

A beautiful inherited estate. Three unforgettable love stories.

Loving Amber

(A standalone novel. Book 1 of The Riverstone Series.)

Torn by tragedy. Reunited by love.

A steamy forbidden romance. Two years following her husband's tragic

death, a widow struggles with feelings for the man she holds
responsible.

"Loving Amber is a second chance at love story with a twist of the
forbidden. This book had so many feels. My heart broke over and over
again." - Sultry Sirens Book Blog

*Author's note: contains sexual scenes and some coarse language. This is the
first book of the Riverstone Estate Series and can be enjoyed as a
STANDALONE read.*

Loving Ruby

(A standalone novel. Book 2 of The Riverstone Series.)

A sinful boss secretary romance.

I've heard all the rumours: He killed his wife. He's on house arrest. He's
a vampire. Yet still, when I get a job offer from the reclusive Mr. Hyde, I
jump at the chance. Yes, I know I'm crazy.

I'm cautious at first, but then I discover a beautiful, quirky man. I also
see a tortured soul who lives in darkness. I know I should run, yet I can't
tear myself away. I want to discover all his secrets. I desperately want to
help him. And when he draws me deeper into his strange little world, I
want to stay.

*Author's note: contains sexual scenes and some coarse language. This is the
second book of the Riverstone Estate Series and can be enjoyed as a
STANDALONE read.*

Loving Jade

(A standalone novel. Book 3 of The Riverstone Series.)

A story about courage and new beginnings.

In an attempt to escape her abusive husband, a woman seeks refuge at a
horse estate and falls in love with her equine therapist.

Author's note: contains sexual scenes and some coarse language. This is the last

The Ground Rules Trilogy

Two beautiful couples. **Five** simple rules. **One** *hot* mess.

Gabe and Mirella Keates are happily married – high school sweethearts, in fact. But by chance, one fateful night, they meet the rich and enigmatic Weston Hanson and his beautiful wife Bridget.

Mirella is instantly drawn to the sexy, mysterious, peculiar man and soon becomes obsessed with him. And when the dynamic couple makes them an unthinkable proposal, Mirella and Gabe accept, driven by lust and desire, despite knowing the risks.

The ground rules are clear, but as Mirella discovers the kind and gentle man hidden under Weston's cold, rigid exterior, she soon falls hard for him. And as Weston's walls begin to crumble, he starts to break his own rules as well.

As Mirella falls deeper, she is torn between her feelings for Weston and her love for her husband. And as the volatile and passionate Gabe becomes increasingly jealous, Mirella realizes her entire world is tearing at the seams.

Author's note: contains sexual scenes and some coarse language. This is a trilogy but the first book can be enjoyed as a standalone read. The Ground Rules (Book 1), The Ground Rules Rewritten (Book 2), The Ground Rules Undone (Book 3)

Read the *excerpt of Chapter One* following this section.

The One Week Series - A series of steamy standalone reads.

One Week

A troubled marriage. A one week hall pass. A married woman falls for a beautiful stranger she meets online, and is given permission by her husband to spend a week with him.

One Week Hating You (Book 2)

One Week in Paris (Book 3)

Stuck with You: A ONE WEEK novella.

ONLY YOU - EXCERPT - CHAPTER ONE

I'm making a complete mess.

Who knew it was so hard to paint polka dots on one's own nails? Other women make this kind of thing look so easy.

But then again, I'm not most women. I'm a "character," my bestie says. That might just be Trish's way of saying *neurotic, irrational... crazy.*

I screw the bottle of black nail polish shut, my pinkie pointed toward the ceiling. My nails look like shit, and I couldn't care less. I'm not going anywhere tonight. I'm probably destined to never go anywhere again. I think I'll just stay home for the rest of my life and watch romantic comedies and take up crocheting again. I used to be really good at it. I'm sure it's like riding a bicycle.

The intercom buzzes. I know it's Trish, so I buzz her up, unlock the door, plop on the sofa, and get back to my laptop. I managed to leave it for a whole ten minutes while I was attempting to art-ify my nails.

Complete fail.

I check out Melanie's page again. I'm obsessed. Ever since the breakup a week ago, I've been fixated on her. I want to see what she has that I don't have. I want to know why Matthew chose her over me. Why he would end a two-year relationship to be with her?

I hate her. I really do. I know it's horrible to hate someone, and I don't think I've ever hated anyone before.

But I *really* do hate her.

It's pretty serious actually. She's been the star in many macabre scenarios I've cooked up—it's amazing what the mind can conjure. Seriously, I think I've missed my calling; a career as a crime fiction novelist might suit me perfectly—it would be a lot more interesting than bookkeeping. One scenario involved the roof of her house collapsing on her. In another, she was shaving her ridiculously long legs in the bath, then her plugged-in hair dryer just happened to fall in. Of course, to my delight, she was fried to bits. I also dreamed up a scenario where she got bit by a black widow. I wonder if we even have poisonous spiders in Vermont. Probably not. Damn, why can't we live in Australia?

To my pleasure (or horror—I'm not sure), all her posts are public, so I can efficiently stalk her. We're not even friends, and she has no clue who I am. Well, that's not quite true. I'm sure she knows something about me—she stole my boyfriend, after all.

There's a new post! And this one takes the cake. This one beats the pic of her new slutty heels. She's eating a three-scoop ice cream cone. Pleeaaase, I'm sure she had a few licks and the cone was trashed as soon as the photo was taken. Ice-cream-eating faker.

Speaking of ice cream, Trish swoops in with a tub of fudge marble—my favorite. She walks straight to the kitchen and tucks it away in my tiny freezer. She shakes her head as she inches closer, then takes a seat next to me on the sofa. "You're stalking her again, I see."

I don't want to admit it, but yes. It's addictive. "Check out the latest photo she posted. She drives a freakin' red Mustang convertible, for crying out loud. I don't even have a car."

"But your beach cruiser is really cool," Trish chirps. "I love the basket... and the little bell."

I roll my eyes and scroll down her feed. "And look at this photo. She's drinking a cool foreign beer and laughing with the boys."

"Well... um..." Trish says, at a loss for words. Then she spots the flashy red shoes with the colorful platform heels. "Oh my God, those shoes are fabulous, and I'm not even into shoes."

I glare at her. "You're not helping."

"I'm sorry," she adds quickly. "I just like the artsy design. That's all. I'm sure she can't even walk in those things."

"You're probably right. I hope she falls and breaks her neck."

"So... you still want her to die, I see," she says with a sigh.

"Yes." I'm not ashamed to admit it—I want her to *die*. I wonder if it's a sin to wish for someone's death, but I don't ponder it too long. "And look..." I point at the photo which got to me the most—a comical heart with the words *I love butt sex.* "And then she wrote, 'Not every week, but once in a while, it's fun to stir shit up.'"

"That's kind of clever," Trish points out with a laugh.

"God, you're not fucking helping. Why don't you go back home and take your tub of ice cream with you?"

"Jeez, I don't think I've ever heard you swear, Sammy," she says, and then she softens her tone. "You're really upset. I don't think I've ever seen you this angry... ever."

Trish is a real friend. I can see it in her eyes—she's just as upset as I am. When you hurt, real friends feel your pain and hurt as much as you do. She pulls me to her and wraps her arms around me. I instantly fall into sobs.

"She's the 'cool girl,'" I cry. "He left me for the fuckin' cool girl."

Trish shakes her head, almost as pissed off as I am. "That's it... do you know where she lives? Let's go beat up that bitch."

"I know where she lives, but she has a black belt in judo. She'd probably beat the shit out of *us*."

"Damn, I'm starting to really hate this bitch. Wait... you know where she lives?"

I shrug. "She's everything I'm not. She's perky and blond, really cool, speaks three languages, and loves anal. How the hell am I supposed to compete with that?"

"Oh, Sammy," she says, pulling from me. She takes my face in her hands. "You don't, sweetie. You don't compete with that. You're completely different than her. You're sweet, quirky, and smart. You're your own person. And if she's the one he's looking for, he obviously wasn't the one for you."

I'm still crying buckets—I just can't help myself. I can't help comparing myself to her. She's all legs and long blond hair, big blue eyes and tiny waist. I'm short with plain brown eyes and hair, and I'd love to lose those last ten pounds. One or two people have told me that I remind them of Selena Gomez, but I'm pretty sure they needed to have their eyes checked.

She stares at me and winces. Her large bohemian earrings clang as she shakes her head. "Damn, I wish I could stay with you this weekend."

I sit up straighter. "It's okay, Trish. I'll be fine, I promise."

"But you're driving yourself crazy. You need to stop stalking her. You're going to go insane."

"I know I should stop. I don't know what's wrong with me."

"You're acting crazy. And honestly, I'm a little afraid that you are actually going to go try to off her," she adds with a shaky little laugh.

It's not funny. Because I *do* feel as if I could really kill the woman.

"Seriously," she says, "you wouldn't do well in prison. They don't have Netflix and chai lattes in prison."

I blow out a breath. "I know... I wouldn't survive."

"I wish I didn't have that art retreat. I want to stay with you."

"But you've been looking forward to it forever," I point out. "I'll be fine."

I know I won't be though. It seems I'm even more upset now than I was last week when Matthew brought me to that fancy restaurant and dumped me. We'd even been planning to set off to Florida this week for a holiday. I had the week booked off work.

At least he had the decency to not lie when I asked him if there was someone else. But now, I wish he had. Then I wouldn't be obsessing over this woman, imagining her with him—kissing, walking hand-in-hand, eating spaghetti like a scene from Disney's *Lady and the Tramp*, and having stupid anal sex.

Trish bounces off the couch. "I have an idea! It's fabulous. I'm not sure why I didn't think about it before."

I stare at her, wide-eyed, wondering what the hell she's going on about.

"You come with me," she almost sings. "Come to the art retreat with me. A week in Québec City, surrounded by French-Canadian hotties, it'll be the perfect distraction. You've already booked the week off work. Your passport is still good, right? It's meant to be."

I stare at her, speechless.

"What?"

"I can't draw to save my life. I don't have a single artistic bone in my body." I stretch out my arms, displaying my hands. "Just look at these nails."

She stares at the mess I've made of my nails and actually winces. "God... what were you trying to do?"

"I was trying to get my nails to look like hers," I explain as I scroll down Melanie's feed. "See?"

She glares at the photo of Melanie's perfect pink and black-polka-dot mani for what seems like eternity. I turn my gaze to the screen and glare too. Fuck her... and her pretty nails. I jerk back when Trish snaps my laptop shut with a loud slap.

"That's it," she scoffs. "No more internet for you. You're coming with me, and I don't want to hear another word. No ifs, ands, or buts about it."

www.ingramcontent.com/pod-product-compliance
Lightning Source LLC
Chambersburg PA
CBHW020339160726
47992CB00004B/1887